handwritten annotations:

Keeping 18
Rowan
med a
Birchvo
Spring
dup
cks

About the author

Sandrea Mosses is a medium, psychic, author, columnist and broadcaster with over thirty years' experience in psychic matters. She has worked as a medium in Canada, Spain, Ireland and the U.K. She has broadcast on both TV and radio. She has worked for twenty years in clearing unwanted psychic phenomena from the lives of families and individuals.

handwritten:

L X K MOU

X Q E S I H

SPZ 0108

Spmue 108

PSYCHIC CHILDREN

SANDREA MOSSES

PSYCHIC CHILDREN

Vanguard Press

A CIP catalogue record for this title is
available from the British Library.

ISBN 978 1 80016 369 0

Vanguard Press is an imprint of
Pegasus Elliot MacKenzie Publishers Ltd.
www.pegasuspublishers.com

First Published in 2022

Vanguard Press
Sheraton House Castle Park
Cambridge England

Printed & Bound in Great Britain

Dedication

David, my husband, for your undying support, and
my best friend Lyn.

Acknowledgements

To all my fellow Ghostbusters who gave their time freely and tirelessly to rid families of darkness and torment. David, Lyn, Karen, Linda, Patrick and Shaune, to name just a few. Thank you. You did make a difference.

Foreword

For twenty years, as a working medium, I have been involved in clearing unquiet spirits and unwanted phenomena from people's homes, and occasionally from commercial and industrial premises. This activity is always undertaken with the assistance of other mediums and psychics, for want of a better expression, a team. The most important assistance is provided by the spirit world.

In the course of conducting this activity, there has necessarily been contact with a considerable number of children. The children have proved fascinating in a number of ways: their reaction to the occurrences, their understanding and interpretation of events, their resilience in the face of the most trying circumstances.

It rapidly became clear to me that some of the children were reacting as they did because they themselves were exhibiting psychic powers, occasionally to a remarkable extent.

This book is a record of these encounters.

Introduction

Many parents will have at least one story to tell where they could not logic out the behaviour of their child. Where the child did or said something that made it obvious that their actions or behaviours could not be explained in a normal way. The child was definitely experiencing something out of the ordinary that could not be explained. Whether this is the presence of an imaginary friend that no one else has ever seen; or maybe their recognition and knowledge of a long gone relative who they are able to describe with fascinating accuracy, often down to their personal habits. Or it could be stories of angels who protect them and look after them, describing their pretty clothes, wings and the colour of their hair.

Some people believe that children maintain their connection with the heavenly realms until they reach the age of seven or eight. This was certainly the belief of the poet Wordsworth, who mentions it in his poem *The Prelude*. From this point on their connection appears to lessen as they become more embroiled in everyday life here on Earth. As they do, they shift their focus away from their heavenly homes and become more focused on day-to-day life. For others, this connection lasts a lot longer.

People often ask how could the spirit realm allow demons, evil spirits, ghosts and such to torment little children? Life here on Earth is too complicated to be able to answer that in one sentence, paragraph or book. One thing we do need to take into consideration is the rule of free will and this is often the deciphering factor that enables these entities to interact with our world. We may inadvertently invite these entities into our home, or the previous occupants may have done so. The rule on non-intervention, unless invited to do so, prevents guides and angels from intervening. What it does not do is stop them from protecting the children through distraction. We also need to allow that children have far greater resilience that we give them credit for.

I have rarely seen a child terrified by such events. I had spoken to parents and heard them say that the child was terrified in the night, but usually they are unperturbed by the presence of the darkest forces. I remember on one occasion talking to two young girls who were around six and nine at the time. They were explaining to me the events that had unfolded around them. This included talking about dolls and a rather sinister looking clown, for the older readers this resembled Chuckie the possessed doll of cinematic fame. In a very matter-of-fact way, they described how the bad man lived inside the clown sometimes, to try and frighten them. 'The clown comes alive. Once it tried to get on to my face and smother me,' the older girl said; she looked at her sister for assurance, who vacantly nodded in agreement. On another occasion, a young boy told me that the ghost sometimes lay underneath the bed trying to frighten him. All so matter-of-fact in their recollection of things. When you questioned these children and talked more, at the same time they would talk of a favourite relative or an angel. It would seem, often the case, that no matter how frightening we find these incidents, these children are protected by relatives who have passed on, who always seem to be present around these events. Children are often reluctant to talk about these visits or the protection they receive and will often change the subject when asked. But there is usually one common factor: they are distracted and protected by these visitations and no matter how horrific the event has been, it appears to have had no lasting stain or impact on them at the time they are recalling these events. This is not to say that when they view the incidents through adult eyes, their values do not shift. Why? Because you would have been afraid, everything about it indicates that they should have been afraid.

I remember talking to two young brothers who lived in a rather ostentatious barn conversion set on contaminated ground. The property was amazing, the energies inside, were remarkable A regular occurrence was for all the drawers and cupboards in their bedrooms repeatedly to open and shut. This would last for several minutes. They calmly told me their deceased granddad, (my words not theirs), had told them to put blue tack on the drawers and doors, as it was the noise that disturbed them. This would quieten down the sound, and hopefully it would not wake them. This is what they had both duly done. The younger boy was experiencing marching soldiers trooping through his bedroom right across his bed. His granddad told him to move his bed so he wouldn't be in the way. I was fascinated. As they shared their stories with me, as they talked, they continued to play with their toy soldiers, not flinching. They might have been telling me about a small kitten disturbing their sleep.

The spirit guardians of children may not be able to stop events happening, but they certainly appear to be able to protect the children so that their recall of events appears to be reduced to no more than an irritation, which in a very short period of time diminishes to nothing.

Children are also the best yardstick for measuring if we have been successful in removing an entity permanently from their lives. I have on more than one occasion asked a child on returning if the house is better now, only to be told the 'nasty man' is hiding in the garage, or, no, he has gone next door and he will be back soon. On one occasion I was told by a very wise little three-year-old that the man was waiting in the house over the road and was watching me: as soon as I went, he would return. It was from this point on, many years ago, that I discovered the importance of sealing the building to stop anything from leaving before we had chance to remove it. Once I was told that the hag was still in the house, sitting on the chair upstairs, waiting for us to go. Or the time we had been to a very difficult clearance, Mom had sent the children to a relative's without telling them what we were about to do. On their return, the youngest daughter ran into the house asking the mom, 'What have you done? She is so angry now, we are all going to suffer. You have tried to get rid of her and she is so annoyed.' The mother was bowled over, how did the child know? The child wasn't told, and the child had not seen us. Yet, she clearly did know and delivered her tale of woe as soon as she was through the front door of the house. Unfortunately, the warning was not heeded, and the entity attacked the eldest daughter that night, blacking both her eyes when she threw a television at her, hitting her full on in the face.

Charlie, Charlie, Come and Haunt Me!

It was the latest children's craze in 2015. Apparently, everyone was talking about it. Charlie, Charlie it was called. Its popularity spread through media attention and the hashtag Charlie, Charlie Challenge, where it was alleged two million people took up the challenge. It was said to be an old Mexican game for calling up a demon, although there does not appear to be any foundation to this. Within a very short period of time, this game was being played in the corner of every school playground. The rules of the game are simple. It involves drawing a grid on four boxes.

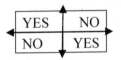

Down the middle axis a pencil is placed. A second pencil is balanced on top of the first one. The first question everyone asks, by speaking to the pencils, is, 'Charlie can we play?' or 'Are you here?' or 'Are you there?' When they finish, they must also seek permission to stop playing. Some people thought the pencil moving was a fluke, and with so many people standing close by, breathing, wind, etc., would move the top pencil to answer the questions. However, other people, experts in board games, such as the Ouija Board, were less relaxed and were greatly concerned. A Ouija Board works by the players focusing their energy onto the planchette.

Now there are two forces at play here.

You are powering the board by lending your energy through your focused attention.

You are giving whoever decided to come through permission to do so. You are in fact inviting them in, without any filters.

The combination of the two is like saying 'free booze party' on social media and leaving the front door wide open for whoever wishes to come and join you. There are no filters of number or suitability of the characters you are inviting in. Some may be very nice, others may not. It is a risk and a gamble. Which most of us would never take.

The principles are the same. The difference is that the majority of the Charlie, Charlie players were vulnerable children, who have given their permission. The innocence of a child is often the sweetest fruit for demonic forces, and no doubt that is what happened here.

But what makes this 'childish game' so dangerous or so effective? How can two pencils enable communications with dark entities? We know that energy lines cross-section the planet, and it is at the grid points that the energy is the strongest. Indeed, a cross symbol is identified as being an integral part of sacred geometry.

It is the crossing of the pencils which is important. The central point between these two items creates a portal. A doorway which is powered through intention and concentration. A doorway which in the right circumstances enables occupants of the lower planes to freely enter into our world. However, these two factors on their own are not enough. It is the invitation to communicate which truly enables the entities to traverse the portal. It is this invitation that lowers the veil, and once the veil is crossed, there is nothing to push or inspire these entities to return to their world. Why return when everything here is more interesting? It is not a level playing field. In fact, the odds are clearly stacked against us. We are competing or being challenged by entities we cannot see, which we do not understand and who are operating in a psychic field which we are unfamiliar with. We do not know the rules, we do not know our opponents or their capabilities and we are not equipped to deal with them. It is game, set and match, but not in our favour.

Sukhi was desperate when she rang me. She was also very angry, as she had always told Thomas not to do this kind of thing. Sukhi was a naturally gifted psychic with a strong clairvoyant skill, she had long suspected her son could see too. For her the death of a very close relative and the conversations she had with Thomas long confirmed this.

When the troubles started at home, Sukhi had no idea that Thomas had been playing Charlie, Charlie. At this stage she had no idea what the game involved. It had swept through the school in days and apparently everyone was playing it. The difficulty with psychically gifted children is that their senses are outside the range of other children. They can reach much higher and unfortunately lower, stretching their seeing and sensing way beyond the spectrum of a normal child. To the etheric world they shine and stand out from others. Unfortunately, this principle applies to both sides, the light, and the darkness. This is why it is imperative that psychically gifted children should be protected as much as possible. The 'other side' recognises this, and most gifted children are born to parents with the gift. This is nothing new. As far back as the Middle Ages, folklore spoke of the seventh child of the seventh child, always said to be gifted, on both sides of the channel and within Celtic history.

The onslaught in the house began very quickly. It was as if a pathway had opened up into their apartment. The only safe zone appeared to be Sukhi's bedroom. Her son, who had always loved his bedroom, was refusing to go into the room, saying it was cold and dark, and for the first time in his life at seven years old he was sleeping in his mom's bedroom All other areas were affected. It started with the sound of someone, or something, running up and down the corridor. To all intents and purposes, it was as if several young children were running noisily up and down the corridor. Sukhi had called the Housing Association several times, as she thought that on top of everything else there was a problem with the drains, as a pungent smell was constantly in the flat, driving Sukhi to distraction. At the same time, they both started to experience terrible dreams, almost bordering on nightmares. What was even more disturbing is that these dreams were almost the same, or very similar in nature. They involved a small clown-like figure, about three feet in height, very solid in build, with a very white skin tone, fixed large dark eyes and sinister painted red cheeks. Its eyes stared at them and never moved. The dreams were always very dark. On one occasion they both dreamt simultaneously they were trapped in a very dark place and could find no way out. They were very afraid, a never-ending nightmare. Slowly this thing would appear from a darkened corner and fade as quickly as it appeared. On another occasion there was a feeling that a recently departed relative was trapped, held by this darkness. These dreams were waking them up in the night. At first, Thomas would run from his little room into Mom's room. Later he was already in her room. Thomas was very fortunate and the benefactor of many relatives. His room was filled to bursting with a lot of toys, including electronic robots. When Mom probed him, it seemed things had started off with the lights on one of the robots flickering in the night. He became diligent in ensuring they were all turned off. Yet the red lights continued to flicker on and off. Over the next couple of weeks, it grew stronger. No flickering, the toys would burst into life, sometimes several at once. Or sinisterly call his name as he frantically tried to run to his mom's bedroom down the hallway.

After one particular night, as a forlorn Thomas sat toying with his breakfast, he asked his mom if she thought this, referring to the events in the apartment, was because he had forgot to ask Charlie if they could end the game. Absentmindedly she agreed, then stopped in her tracks. 'Who is Charlie, babe?' she asked. The story slowly unfolded over breakfast, and that night. It would seem Thomas was, for once, the most popular child in his year. The children were all playing Charlie, Charlie in the playground, and when Thomas was part of the game it always worked with excellent results. It would appear that at a game a couple of weeks ago, the break had been abruptly ended by the ringing of the bell, mid-game. They had forgotten to ask Charlie if they could stop playing. No one else appeared to be having any problems but Thomas. Sukhi was shocked. This was the first she had heard of this sinister game. She understood the dangers of games like this. Her first port of call was the school to inform them of the dangers of this type of activity. They were sympathetic and instructed all children to stop, staff presence in the play areas was increased. This was easy to implement as the interest in the game was fading somewhat.

But the activity in Sukhi's home was increasing. The apartment was less than five years old, the kitchen and lounge were open plan. To top it all, her curtains in the lounge were turning black with mould. Yet the Housing Association could find no damp readings through the apartment. It had now installed monitors throughout the property to try and discover what was happening. At the same time, it was tracing the sewers to see if there was a leak somewhere.

The kitchen and bathroom and toilet had no windows. This means there is no natural flow of energy, it will become trapped. The whole Estate sits on former mining works, adjacent to where a huge factory and slaughterhouse once sat that sent millions of animals to their deaths. The desecration of the land and the fear generated from this slaughterhouse were enough to create some very unpleasant energies and gateways. In the short period of time, in the housing complex there had been a lot of reports of paranormal activity on the site. Considering the energetic contamination of this area, this was no great surprise.

I myself was ignorant of the Charlie, Charlie game before the call. Within two hours I was very au fait with it and the ramifications of playing it. I accepted the case, and off Lyn, Shaune and I set in search of the apartment. It really was quite difficult to find, and we were driving around to no avail and, guess what, none of us had signal, all on different networks. It knew we were coming. I looked across, and there sat a lone cat, underneath a window staring out towards our direction, it was as if it was watching us drive slowly up the road. 'There it is,' I said.

'How do you know?' they both asked. I pointed to the cat, no need for words and quite rightly so, it was the property. I cannot tell you the times animals have helped me, and today was no exception.

We were now late. An anxious Sukhi met us at the door, Thomas had been packed off to his dad's. Sometimes it helps to have children in the property, other times it doesn't. It didn't feel right on this occasion, so we removed him from the apartment. Besides, how he reacted when he returned would be a barometer of our success, confirmation for Sukhi that her home was safe.

Darkness is always present when something is overshadowing a house. This was no exception. What was more noticeable was the pungent smell, like rotting flesh. This would prove to be quite difficult to work against, but we were equally determined as this thing was causing untold damage. Lyn and Shaune were working blind. They knew of the game, but not the activity. This would be the confirmation when we had it in our sights. Without a doubt, the darkest room was the bedroom occupied by Thomas. We all noticed almost immediately that the corner of the kitchen seemed much lower than the rest of the apartment. It was as if it was at least three feet lower than the other end of the room.

As if something was trying to tell us, be mindful of the land. We would be.

As we stood, ping, off went the light bulb. This was almost a daily occurrence, Sukhi had a bag full of them. 'They are checking the electrics as well,' she said. She rolled her eyes and we all smiled, we knew what was going on. As we stood in the living room, there was a strange sound coming from Thomas's bedroom. It was like a toy turning on and off. Sukhi showed us that all the electronic toys had their batteries removed. Lyn and Shaune were drawn directly to the robots, especially the one that had had been making the noise and turning its lights on. It was as if something was looking at us from the toy. A further sound could be heard in the bathroom, then the living room. We now had had enough distractions. Time for action.

In the corner of the room both Lyn and Shaune described the tormentor of Sukhi and Thomas's dreams. It was actually inside one of the robots, trying to disguise itself. The robot appeared to transform. We could physically see it with our eyes. A fixed smile, white skin tone and dark staring eyes could be detected psychically and almost physically. Collectively we described this 'thing'. It had underestimated us and knew it, this thing did not expect us to find it. Within seconds a strong blast of air shot between us. It was as if someone or something had run in between us. We all noticed it and collectively said so. 'Wow, what was that?' said Shaune.

'Look,' Lyn said. 'It's gone.' She was correct, the robot was now a robot. We chased this rapid little 'thing' around the flat, until we finally trapped it in the bathroom. By now it had shrunk down to inches in size. This was not of this world. It was the strangest thing we had ever encountered. The thing itself appeared robotic; it was almost gnome-like in its features. Within moments we had it trapped, cornered, and together deftly shifted it from one energetic zone to another.

What was it?

The school was not far away, again set on former mining works. The Charlie, Charlie game had opened a doorway to these mines. Since mining began, there have been stories, of demons, Gnomes, Fairies, Tommy Knockers, etc., who are said to either help or hinder the miners. Many miners followed an extensive list of dos and don'ts so as not to stir the anger in these creatures who were thought to have the powers to create fatal falls in the mines that could deny them their work or take their lives.

Here we encountered one of these creatures.

Once the property was cleared and cleansed, life slowly returned to normal, and Thomas never again attempted to play the game. This gifted little boy knew what had been conjured up. He explained to Sukhi it was a strange creature, as it refused to talk. It was almost as if it had been sent to cause havoc against its will, like a wind-up toy put into action. As soon as Thomas returned, he carefully entered and scanned each room.

Only then would he confirm with his mom that the 'thing', as he called it, had gone. Although it was quite a while before he would have another toy robot in his room, let alone put any batteries in.

The Barn in the Attic

Leila was old beyond her years. When I met her at a local spiritualist church, I didn't think for one minute that she was only sixteen years old. She looked much older and had the confident air of someone in her early twenties. She had been psychically gifted from childhood and was drawn to anything spiritual. This is how she became a member of the spiritualist church. I'm not quite sure how, on that very busy night, I came into conversation with her, but I did. As soon as I began to talk to her, several people around her prompted her to tell me about the problems at home.

It seemed that the main problem activity was in the bedrooms in the attic, although disturbances had occurred throughout the house. A dark shadow was seen ascending and descending the stairs. A further darkness had been seen in the hallway and kitchen. Her brother had fallen asleep downstairs and had woken to feel something inches from his face, pressing down on him. This sinister event was similar to a scene from one of the *Alien* films, when the Alien stands with its face inches from Sigourney Weavers.

The experience wasn't just limited to the lounge. Another brother had woken to a similar experience in his top bunk. Yet another brother had fallen down the narrow stairs on several occasions. Leila herself was often really afraid in her bedroom and was convinced something was watching her. She could also feel someone in the room, and whoever it was, exuded a feeling of utter fear. Bangs and scratching sounds came from empty cupboards. Over the years the family had been subjected to an array of things. Everyone but Dad had been subjected to some unearthly incident. Yet he remained unconvinced.

Martin, Lyn, Paul and I joined our vibrations together as always before entering into the property. The giant flat screen television was blasting away, and a reluctant father agreed to turn it off, and keep it turned off for the duration of our visit. The vibration in the whole house was one of feeling uncomfortable, not welcome, is the easiest way to describe it. Paul complained of feeling trapped. The only place free of this suppressive atmosphere was the conservatory. Here the atmosphere felt normal. Clean and fresh. It lacked the darkness that appeared to prevail through the whole of the house.

The attic had been converted. It now housed two further bedrooms, which we accessed via other rooms. This change had been completed a significant length of time ago to accommodate the five children, and to give them their own personal space. We decided to start in Leila's room. As we traversed the rooms with the bunks in, the atmosphere was so suppressive it was almost difficult to breathe. You certainly didn't want to stay in this room any longer than necessary. We climbed the narrow staircase into Leila's room. The room was very tiny and barely able to hold all of us. In fact, the clearance was conducted with me standing halfway up the stairs and Mom at the foot of the stairs.

None of us was prepared for what met us in this room. This tiny room had little natural light. As we ascended into the room, it was as if we had entered the upper part of a seventeenth-century barn. The whole room had a strong sense of being a barn, not a bedroom. A feeling that you were hiding in the rafters, and with one wrong move you would fall, surely to your death. The room felt incredibly cold and as we stood there it was as if history was re-playing itself. Here we were hiding in a barn, hiding from Roundhead soldiers. Somehow, the former barn had become entangled with the current period and the two were as one. This room felt and smelt like a barn.

There in the corner was a man, a soldier. He was trapped in this etheric imprint, and he still thought the Roundheads were coming to get him. He traversed from room to room, intimidating everyone and everything that came into his pathway. He thought he was fighting for his life, and he had had many years to develop his skills. His main weapon was fear, and he was using anything he could to frighten this family, who he saw as the foe.

We decided to push him through to the other room, which was a little bigger and easier to work in. So we moved over to the other room. Martin and Lyn were the first to climb the narrow staircase. As I gingerly climbed up, I felt as if something was trying to push me down, and it was taking me all my time to hold onto the stairs and secure my footing. I stopped for a moment 'Has anyone fallen down these stairs?' I asked Leila.

'Yes, my brother, several times,' she replied.

'I'm not surprised,' I said.

'Why,' she asked? I explained how I could feel someone trying to wrong-foot me on the stairs and push me off. Leila said everyone just thought her brother was clumsy, although she did add, he had fallen down on numerous occasions. Sober or not!

Whatever was trying to knock me down, I pushed to the side and made sure he stopped there. We entered into the room, and it was exactly the same as Leila's, this strong feeling of being in a barn, high up in the eaves, a suppressive and fear-inducing sensation. As we tuned in, we could see a huge vortex, a doorway on the energy grid system. Somehow, when these houses were built where the former barn had stood, some kind of fault had occurred, and these two worlds became entwined together. Unfortunately for Leila and her family, their property stood on the precise point where the small room in the eaves had been constructed, this was now manifesting into their world. This angry entity could not leave, and the family were being tormented.

As I suspected, the family and families before them had been tormented. This energy node was huge. We would shut that later. Now our focus was on this man and sending him back where he belonged.

We closed in the room to contain him is this space. He then began moving in close to each and every one of us. He rushed directly up then appeared to grow three times in size and towered above us. He then shrank back down and darted towards the next victim. This he continued to do all the time. We could not communicate with him, it was impossible, he was too angry. Years of being held in this location seemed to have unhinged his soul. He was completely dark, hellbent on revenge and protecting himself, it was impossible to communicate with him. It was as if his soul had lost its human side and turned into some kind of monster. We had had enough. We brought the sides of the room in, using a visualisation of silver walls, until we had boxed him into a very, very small space. We then opened a doorway above his head, we ethereally entered into his makeshift prison and began raising him up and pushing him through this doorway. We did not try to communicate or comfort him, or tell him to look for a loved one. It was useless, a waste of energy, we merely pushed him through. The 'other side' would be waiting for him, they would cleanse him and re-build him. But looking at the state of this deranged soul, this was going to take an awful long time. But then again, he had a lot of time.

But restore him through love and cleansing they would, until he was back to his self again.

We then turned our energy to the large vortex. This was not a positive node, it was churning out black spirals of energy that filled the house and no doubt the properties on either side of it.

We concentrated our energies on shutting down this node, it was huge. It extended high into the roof space of this house. It passed down, capturing the main staircase, hallway, lounge and the bedroom with the bunks in on the way, with a small amount in the kitchen. In fact, it spread across every room where the family had seen or heard things. With huge slabs of silver energy, we pushed down, until we had closed off the opening. We pushed and pushed until there were no signs of it in the house. Then deep in the bowels of the Earth we capped it with light. We then scanned and checked again to ensure it was closed, gone forever; closing this bridge between the etheric world and ours forever.

We then set about cleansing the whole of the house of the stagnant vibrations which seemed to hang in the ether of nearly every room. Built up over time, these spread a heavy suppressive atmosphere throughout the whole dwelling. In minutes it began to lift, it felt lighter, it looked lighter. More light seemed to fill every room and at last normality appeared to be returning to the house.

Even the father who did not believe commented on how light and fresh the house felt. The difference it made, we all had to agree, was astounding. Afterwards, we couldn't help but comment, we didn't know how people managed to live, relatively unharmed, in these suppressive places, but they did, because they did not know any better.

Already Moved On

As we pulled up in front of the old end-terrace house, there appeared to be no sign of life at all in there. By now it was nine o'clock at night, the nights were drawing in, yet the house was in complete darkness. Alongside the house stood a large car park, serving a large social club, which was set back from the road. Patrick had arrived on his own, and Lyn, Paul and I were car-sharing. We quickly got out of the car, and immediately sealed the property to ensure that whatever was there was not going to escape. After seeing the property, we looked at each other; we could see directly into the house and it was clear no one was there. We checked the time, but before I had chance to reach for my phone and call, three very nervous-looking girls emerged from the adjacent car park.

'Are you Sandrea?' one of the girls asked rather nervously. Smiling I explained, yes, I was Sandrea, I then went on to introduce Lyn, Paul and Patrick.

'Which one of you is Emma?' I asked.

'I am,' answered one of the girls nervously. She then added, 'This is Jodie, my sister, and Claire, my sister-in-law.' She then added, 'I hope it was okay to bring them along with me, only I am really nervous and afraid to go back in the house.'

'Yes, that is fine,' I said.

Emma went on to explain that since I had spoken to her four days ago, she had moved out. Neither she nor her sister could bear to be in the property for another day. Emma and Jodie had lived with Emma's two-year-old son, in the property for approximately five months. Both Emma and Jodie's parents had died quite tragically within eight weeks of each other. Following their death, the girls had taken over the tenancy of their former home. However, trouble with their neighbours resulted in their leaving their former home very quickly. Such was the drive to get away from the drunken neighbours, they had taken the first property they had seen. Their relief at being away from their disruptive neighbours, soon gave way to a fear of the new house they were living in. On reflection, things had not seemed as they should. The house had shown all the classical signs of occupancy by an unseen force. The house was constantly cold, no amount of heating seemed to warm it up. Even on a summer's day, the house always appeared chilly. Each room had the strongest lightbulbs available on the market, with subsidiary lamps present in every room, and yet the rooms seemed to be dull and dark. The house consisted of three bedrooms on the upper floor, with the dining room, lounge, galley kitchen and toilet and bathroom on the ground floor. The lounge, front and rear bedroom appeared to be the worst of them all. Emma slept in the front bedroom, with her son. The room had a small en suite shower and toilet. The tiny box room was vacant, and her sister Jodie slept in the back bedroom, above the lounge.

Within a few months of being in the house, the feelings of being uncomfortable began to increase. At the same time, a series of other problems was beginning to arise. Night-time appeared to be when all the activity began. Jodie could hear constant scratching noises coming from the lounge downstairs. Their mother's beloved Welsh dresser was covered in small scratches. Yet both were baffled where the scratches were coming from. Jodie had on several occasions thought she could hear a woman crying, and she was convinced that her mother was upset that they had failed to look after her Welsh dresser. Emma found that her sleep was being disturbed several times a week. On one occasion she woke to see a hunched figure with red eyes staring at her from the shower room. Her son's toys would disappear, only to reappear several days later, in the precise spot where they had gone missing. Emma's son also began to talk about the horrible man; in childish language he talked of a nasty person who kept waking him during the night, and who stood on the stairs.

The final thing which had tipped Emma and Jodie over the top had been waking up in the middle of the night to the strong smell of burning. Acrid smoke could be smelt throughout the house. Both had woken in absolute terror, convinced a fire had broken out in the house. It was only after an age of searching that they realised there was no fire, and it was difficult to understand where the smell had originated from.

It was this incident that sent Emma and Jodie in search of me and my team.

Emma, sensing our curiosity, went on to explain that her and Jodie felt unable to sleep in the house any more until the problem was solved. Such was their fear that they had sat in the car waiting for us, rather than go back into the house.

As we walked from room to room, we decided that the presence was stronger in the lounge, on the stairs and in the two main bedrooms than anywhere else in the house. Despite being a warm day followed by a relatively warm evening, the house was biting cold. As I pulled my coat closer, I was glad that I had brought it with me that night. Past experience had taught me not to rely on the weather and to expect the worst in terms of temperature on clearing properties. In the lounge, Jodie pointed to the scratches which had mysteriously appeared on her mother's dresser. It looked as if someone had taken a coin and scratched the surface in dozens of places. These were not accidental knocks or abrasions. They looked like someone had deliberately and intentionally gouged at the wood, in some places the scratches were superficial, in others deep cuts covered the surface.

As we walked up the stairs, we ignored the overbearing presence that tried to block our way. We walked from room to room, and as we did, we could actually smell remnants of burning. There was a distinct acrid smell, which permeated across all three rooms and the landing. 'Can you smell it?' Emma asked, as she looked at us all individually.

'Yes, I can,' I said. At the same time Paul, Lyn and Patrick nodded in unison. Yes, we could all smell it. It seemed to fade in and out, yet we could still smell smoke.

Patrick opened the window to see if the smell was coming from outside the property. He shook his head and turned to me and said, 'There is no smell outside, try it yourself. As soon as you put your head outside the smell fades.' He beckoned for us all to see for ourselves, but there was no need. I didn't need any convincing, I felt sure, that there was no earthly source to this smell. Whatever was haunting this house was creating the smoke smell. We would find out why in a little while, but in the meantime, we strolled from room to room, determined to pin down the cause of this family's distress.

Finally, I decided that the energy was strongest in the lounge. So we began to tune in. I could sense a man in his late forties. This man felt so angry, not at the family here, but at his situation. He was so frustrated. This had not happened in the last couple of months, this had built up over a period of time. With each change of tenant, he grew more and more powerful. This was a trapped soul, someone who did not and could not see the

41

doorways that would free him from this hell. In some ways he still felt he belonged to the living. With each new tenant he became more fearful, and he made his presence known to each tenant. What was more frustrating was that the landlord knew the problems, yet he just kept letting the property out.

This man looked old for his age. His face seemed craggy and lined and the effect of years of alcohol abuse and tobacco had taken its toll. This man did not appear to have any connections with this family. His link was with the house. I could sense the acrid smell of an electrical fire. This was how he had died years ago, and he had been incarcerated in this house ever since. I saw the scene: a fire had broken out, caused by a fault in the electrical wiring, he had died in his bed, unaware of the fire and here he remained ever since. This was now going to be quite easy and straightforward. First, we needed to hear his story, and then to convince him that he was dead and it was safe to go through the open doorway. I turned to the others and asked if they could sense anything? If possible, the room had begun to go even colder. You could see the fear in Emma and Jodie as they sensed a change in the room. 'I'm sorry, but this is frightening me,' Emma said, her voice quivering as she spoke. 'It's getting colder,' she added, hysteria beginning to creep into her voice. Jodie, her sister, moved closer to her and Claire placed a comforting arm around her. The cold seemed to rush around the room, and a distinct draft could be felt around us all. I moved the girls into the middle of the circle.

'Do you want to continue?' I asked. 'Remember, it cannot harm you and you only have to put up with this for another ten minutes, then it will be gone forever,' I added.

'I know,' Emma said, nodding her head. 'Please carry on,' she whispered.

I turned to Lyn, Paul and Patrick 'Well? Can you see or sense anything?' Lyn was the first to respond, without trying to alarm the others, she pointed to the corner of the room. This is precisely where this man was standing.

'I sense a man,' Patrick added, and Paul agreed, nodding his head in the same direction to indicate something by the window.

I began tuning into this lost soul. This was precisely what we had here, a lost, frightened soul, who was trapped in his own living hell. Unfortunately, as he tried to reach out, he terrified everyone he came into contact with. I sensed a lonely, frightened soul, living in a rundown, poorly maintained house. He was so glad that someone could now communicate with him, this appeared to be overcoming his fear. Together Lyn and I chatted to him. He was sorry for the distress over the Welsh dresser, he was trying to write, Help me. We listened to his story and between us, we began to show him the light. We sensed a doorway opening up close to the window, and we could feel the presence of his mother beginning to show herself to him. In the doorway stood a short, stocky woman, with salt and pepper hair and a soft glowing complexion. 'Pete, Pete,' she whispered, as she beckoned him to the door. You could feel the energy beginning to lift as the light filtered in through this portal.

'What's happening?' Emma whispered.

'It's okay, Emma, Peter's mother is here, and she is calling him home,' I said. Silently we all began to encourage Pete to go to the light and to his loving mother. You could feel his terror. Still, we gently kept encouraging him to move towards his mother, gently nudging him along. You could feel his attention turn to his mother, and in a moment, he was swathed in her love. He recognised it immediately and almost began to melt. Without a backwards glance, he moved towards the light. As her energy began to permeate the room, a soft warm glow began to illuminate the room, as the darkness and fear began to subside. Slowly she continued to pull him towards her. In a moment he was gone. Instantaneously the doorway folded in on itself and was gone. Yet the warmth and light remained.

'Oh my God, can you feel that?' Emma asked, looking quickly between Claire, Jodie and us. Both Jodie and Claire in utter amazement agreed. 'Does it feel warmer?' Emma added. Through smiling faces they all agreed, the room was warmer and brighter. Emma remained amazed for several minutes and her joy was shared by the others.

We quickly exchanged the energy in each of the rooms and returned the house to normal.

As we sat afterwards in the pub for our customary debrief, we reflected on the plight of this man. I couldn't help but feel a trifle miffed with the landlord. He knew something was wrong with this property. He could not hold a tenant for more than six months, yet he had put profit first, rather than trying to sort out the problem.

Castles and Black Magic

Coincidentally, Gill's daughter, like myself, also worked in healthcare, in a local neighbouring hospital. She worked alongside Andrew. Such were the tales he told her, the deeply concerned daughter relayed them to her mother. And this is how Andrew found us. Andrew and his wife lived with four children from a previous marriage, and one disabled child between them. They could not believe their luck when they found this house, a modern end-terrace with four bedrooms. Within a couple of weeks, they soon realised why the house had been sold £20,000 below the market rate. Neither had it caused concern that the previous owner had already moved out of the property. They were later to discover that the property had had six owners in six years.

The list of problems was endless. The youngest, the daughter who spent most of her time in her small wheelchair, would at times scream in absolute terror, pointing and writhing to get away from some unseen force. An orange orb was seen floating around the house with what seemed to be a child's face inside of it. Putrid smells would fill the house. Huge faces were captured on a DS (electronic device). Andrew spent nearly six hours scanning and checking the photographs on the

DS, to see if somehow they had been overlaid, looking for another reason for these huge visually challenging faces. There was nothing vaguely like them to be found anywhere on the device.

After a short period of time, things seemed to get much worse. The shower had burst into flames at the same time that Andrew was trapped inside the cubicle. The incident nearly killed him. Despite being relatively young, his health had begun to deteriorate with a list of different complaints. A huge amount of salt had been added to his fish tank, killing all his marine fish. As stupid as it sounded, he was convinced this thing was trying to kill him. He was relatively fit, but within a short period of being in the house he developed a heart problem and was reliant on medication to regulate his heart. He was convinced something, somehow, had hidden his medication, only to suddenly reappear. He was a very logical man, but after twelve months in this house all logic had gone out of the window.

I had heard enough to know that we had a serious problem on our hands. So we gathered together at five o'clock, and we set off to Tamworth, aided by the wonderful device, Sat Nav.

The property was situated in a modern development, where access roads were situated to the rear of the properties. We arrived shortly before dusk, and in the dim light, we struggled to find the house and the front door. Eventually we arrived, slightly later than we wanted to. As agreed, both Andrew and his wife were present in the property. The children were with the grandparents, as advised by those above. As we walked into the property, you could sense the worry and concern from both Andrew and Claire. Andrew explained that he had discussed our coming with his wife. When he did so, there had been a wild response. A menacing atmosphere had entered into the room, really frightening them both. They could almost see it spread across the room, like a slow-moving black cloud. The realisation that whatever it was could hear and respond to their conversations had totally freaked them both out. We offered reassurances, that unfortunately this was not normal. But we promised not to leave until we had removed whatever was bothering them.

As we walked into the lounge, the darkness and stench were the two things that hit you, it was repulsive. The anxious couple could see our discomfort and began apologising. Andrew explained it came and went randomly and there was no apparent cause or reason for it. They had spent a fortune bringing professionals in to find the source, all to no avail. The atmosphere was dark and oppressive. I found it hard to understand how these people had managed to sit in this energy day after day. Claire looked at me and shook her head saying, 'It's horrible, but what can we do, we can't afford to move.' She then went on to say everything had gone wrong since they moved in. Even their finances had taken a plunge, trapping them in this hell.

We didn't need to look to find the problem, we could feel it, in every corner of the house, its presence could be felt. I tuned in. Immediately I could see tunnels under the ground, secret passageways leading from ancient buildings, including a castle. The tunnels may be long gone but the energy lines remained in place. I could see stagnant water, pooling underneath the property, thick dark green sludge. There was not one entity, but several, and this was not something that had simply slipped through the veil. This was darkness which had been called up, fetched from the bowels of the earth, for evil purposes. Demons raised through black magic, probably in the Middle Ages. I turned to Andrew and the others and said, I can feel tunnels and caverns running under this property. Lyn agreed, pointing to the route, which was precisely where I had seen it. We were about thirty miles from home, with little or no knowledge of the area. Not knowing our location in relation to the castle, I turned to Andrew. I told him I felt these tunnels were linked to medieval buildings, possibility an Abbey and the castle. Both Andrew and Claire nodded in agreement. Andrew explained that we were not far from the castle and tunnels did run from it. Some were still present and accessible today. He further confirmed that it was thought that an old Abbey had stood within the vicinity of the house. This all made sense. I then explained to Paul, Lyn, Kevin and Patrick that I thought this was entities conjured up through black magic. The smile on

Patrick's face told me that is precisely what he thought. The others nodded in agreement. We knew the source, now we had to pin it down and try to remove it. No wonder I had brought an extra team member tonight, I thought.

We walked around the house, highlighting areas we didn't like, and pin-pointing places to which we needed to return. This was a really spacious house with a huge conservatory, no wonder Andrew and Claire could not believe their luck to get such a large property so cheaply.

We decided to start off in the bedrooms. The girls' room was our first port of call. A wonderful pink room, with a large alcove, shielded off with pretty hanging beads. As we walked into the room, a breeze moved past us. It was as if we had stepped into a room with a large fan running. It hit the curtain and the beads began to bang together, making a ringing sound. 'Does this happen often?' I asked. Claire explained she had never witnessed this before, but all three girls continually complained this is what happened on a regular basis. We scanned the room, the same darkness was present, despite the pink and silver décor. Our attention was drawn to the alcove. The energies were dark and intimidating. There was a small concentration of dark, prickly energy. It had contracted itself into the shape of a small dark ball, about two feet in height. It gave the impression of being harmless, yet its dark sinister red eyes gave it away. Claire confirmed that her daughters had described the exact same image to her. Lyn looked steadily at me and said, 'This is not friendly,' stating the obvious. I nodded in agreement, so did all the others. We had it trapped, it had nowhere to go. So collectively we battered it with light until it did not have enough fight left in it to resist. Immediately the dark dank atmosphere was replaced by a wonderful light which illuminated the whole room. The couple could not believe the difference. We now needed to find the rest of them.

Next, we entered the couple's bedroom. You could feel a dark vortex of energy extending up from the kitchen, right through the matrimonial bed. I strongly suspected something from downstairs had been feeding off the sexual energy, draining the couple of their own life force at the same time. It had created this opening in just the right spot to ensure it could harvest energy for its own purposes. We closed down the opening and replaced the energy in the room using a variety of different techniques. We would worry about the source later when we made our way downstairs.

Next, we entered into the small, boys' room. This was a single room, with a set of bunk beds in. It was smaller than the girls' room, but there were three of them in there opposed to two here. Slowly we made our way down the space between the wall and the bunk beds, I was the last in. So far this was the worst. I couldn't help but ask how these boys had managed to live in this room for twelve months. You could feel the oppression. I could barely breathe, it was as if the air in the room was being sucked out. It was taking me all my time to breathe. Patrick also complained he couldn't breathe. Kevin, looking round the room, decided, like me, that this was the worst of all the rooms. We decided to waste no more time, although it felt we were working through a black fog, which made it difficult to focus. So dark was this room, the bulb seemed unable to illuminate it. As we tuned in, without warning a huge black entity rose up above the top bunk and hit me with a wave of energy. I was caught off guard, it threw me against the wall and held me, pinned to the wall for a few seconds. I saw huge emerald-green eyes form inside this blackness and a mouth roared with energy, which held me in place. With an almighty effort, I broke free from this black form. Before I could do anything, it hit me again and the same happened: I was knocked across the room and pinned against the wall. The group needed no prompting from me. Lyn swung into action, and through her guidance the group collectively hit this entity with everything they could conjure up. This entity knew what was going to happen and had decided to strike first. It was intelligent enough to know who to go for, but it didn't reckon on what we were able to throw at it to bring about its demise. After a five-minute battle, it was gone. Banished back to hell, from where it originated.

We were not convinced that our work was finished, we were all under the opinion that there were more of this. And we were right. Downstairs in the kitchen which sat directly below the matrimonial bed, we found another. Not quite as powerful as the last, but still incredibly powerful. Claire reported it was here that she felt very uncomfortable when cooking. She described feeling as if something was watching over her, as if she could feel a presence, alongside her, which frightened the life out of her. It was here where the fish tank had sat, right in the middle of the former vortex. The fish were obviously interfering with the harvesting of energy, so in a very cruel way, this darkness had killed them, by somehow salinating the water. We wasted no time, we cornered it and beat it with light, until again it did not have the strength to resist.

Finally, we returned to the living room. Here we had a much smaller black blob, like the one in the children's bedroom. Within minutes it was scooped off through the veil. Such was the darkness of this house, we used a variety of different techniques to breakdown the residual energy. Two hours later the light began to shine through in every room.

I heard later that the house remained quiet. The spell was broken, their finances began to recover and they were able to sell the property in a few months and leave behind this hellhole forever.

Chasing You

Hannah's problems had begun seven years ago, when she had moved with her husband into their first home. They were so pleased to be able to afford a three bedroomed house, which incidentally they had gotten at a bargain price. There was no chain, and the buyer moved out long before the sale was complete. Almost immediately their troubles began. Hannah started to suffer from terrible nightmares, where a dark shadow would jump onto her chest, here it would form an outline of a figure and it would try to strangle her. She would wake up screaming and gasping for breath. Both David and Hannah would have put this down to a nightmare, if it wasn't for the red marks and bruising, which could be clearly seen on her neck almost immediately after. These would stay for days. Unable to stand these dreams any longer, Hannah sought the services of a medium. After a thirty-minute session, the medium assured Hannah she had removed whatever it was, and it would never be able to bother her again. And true to her word, the nightmares stopped. Six months later David and Hannah moved house with their two young children, to a tied cottage, which was part of David's job as caretaker to a large house. Set in its own grounds the cottage was wonderful. Surprisingly for its age, this was a spacious three-bedroomed property, with all rooms leading directly off a large hall, which meant the couple could observe their children from every room.

Within a couple of months, Jake the three-year-old was complaining of a little girl called Sasha who kept waking him up during the night. At first the couple dismissed it, but when they returned from their annual holiday, Jake immediately complained of her presence, pleading with his mom and dad to make her go away. It was this break away from their home which convinced the couple that this was not the child's imagination. Something or someone was disturbing his sleep, and he was beginning to get upset about it, refusing to go into his own bed at night and waking up during the night. Their suspicions were further aroused when David woke during the night to see Jake standing in the bedroom. He jumped out of bed, only to find Jake fast asleep in bed. He was sure he had seen his son standing there. And if it wasn't Jake, who was it?

I listened to Hannah's story, and the part about the nightmares. Hannah was convinced that this had long gone, and there was no connection between her experience and what was happening to them now.

Kevin, Patrick, Lyn and I compared diaries, and with several compromises, we found we were all free the following Sunday: so off we set. I had asked Hannah to keep Jake in the house so I could have a chat with him and find out what was happening. Even dealing with a child of three, experience had taught me, with the help of the other side, he would be able to convey to me all I needed to know to trap this entity and push it over to the other side. As we arrived, an anxious Hannah was standing in wait for us. As we walked into the hallway, I could sense a huge vortex in the middle of the area. This stretched deep down into the ground and rose high up in the hallway. As soon as I spoke, Hannah smiled and said, 'That is exactly what my mom says, she is convinced there is something here in this hallway. Everyone comments about it and most people try to skirt round it, rather than crossing it,' she added. You could physically feel it, as you moved your hand across the area, it changed and was quite distinct, a buzzing, tingling vibration could be felt. You could almost draw a line around where it started and finished. I turned to Hannah and said, 'This hallway sits directly over an opening; this is either an old well or a mine shaft, but there is definitely a manmade shaft that leads down into the ground here.' The others nodded their heads in agreement. With this discovery we thought we were halfway to solving the problem. Pleased I had found this so early in the visit, I followed Hannah into the living room to meet David, Jake and the baby who was six months old. The baby was absolutely fascinated with me; he could not take his eyes off me. But he wasn't looking at me; he was looking at White Feather who was standing to my right. Every time I moved slightly his eyes darted towards my side and that is how he remained for the next ten minutes. Hannah introduced me to Jake and asked him to answer me. I sat down alongside him, trying not to frighten him. 'Jake, tell Sandrea all about Sasha.' This was the name he had for the little girl. 'Hello Jake,' I said. 'Is it true, does someone come and visit you in the night?' As I spoke, I smiled gently at him. Shyly he nodded his head. 'Does she come very often?' I asked, trying not to use the phrase little girl, after seeing the doorway in the hall, I was not at all convinced it was a little girl.

As we spoke, the others stood stock still, smiling but feeling the vibrations of the cottage in preparation for our evening's work. 'What colour is she, Jake?' I pressed on.

'Blue,' he replied. Hannah added that this was what he always said.

'What colour is her skin?' I asked.

'Blue,' he replied immediately. He was now beginning to relax, at this tender age he realised, he had someone here who could see what he could see.

'What colour are her eyes?' I added.

'Red,' he said, as quick as a flash. That was precisely what I could see. A most strange figure. About the size of a seven-year-old child. This creature wore no clothes at all and was blue from head to foot, apart from bright red eyes, which had no whites or visible pupils.

'Where is she now?' I asked.

'In my bedroom,' he replied. 'But she wants to go home to her mommy and daddy now.' Hannah explained he was always saying that. I knew instantaneously we had something that was trapped here. It was using Jake as a means to try and convey its dilemma to anyone who would listen. What bothered me was, what had trapped it and what was keeping it captive in these realms? As the evening unfolded, all this would come to light. In the meantime, we needed to track down this demon, which was holding this creature so tightly in our realm.

We began in the children's bedroom. The energy wasn't right, but I couldn't feel anything. I stopped for a moment and went back to talk to Jake, leaving the others to read the vibrations of the building. 'Sorry to trouble you, Jake,' I said, 'but I wonder if you could help me, please?' I asked. 'I am looking for Sasha, could you tell me where she is?'

Without a moment's hesitation he pointed to the corner of the lounge. 'She is over there now.' That is precisely what I thought had happened. She had fled from the bedroom for a reason. Now I had her energy, I could deal with her later. In the meantime, now we needed to find out exactly what it was that was tormenting this family, and probably anyone else who had ever lived in this house. Or was it something that was following the family? We would soon find out.

We moved back into the hallway and decided to shut down this vortex, in fear that whatever was here would merely drop down into it, or even more frighteningly, it would pull something through to help it beat us. So we began to minimise the impact of this vortex, by slowly dropping layer after layer of slabs of solid light onto it. We then sealed it, we could shift it over later, but in the meantime, we were merely concentrating on closing the opening. We walked from room to room. Without doubt it was the parent's bedroom which appeared to hold the strongest vibration.

You could feel the presence as you walked in. We began tuning in and asserting our power, sending waves of light vibration through the darkness, which sat right in the middle of their bed. The room was sealed, it was us versus this darkness and both parties were determined to win.

It was difficult to breathe, as if some force was trying to cut off the supply of air to the room. Patrick spoke first, 'I can't breathe,' he said. 'I'm really struggling here.'

I had to agree with him. It was as if it knew I was asthmatic, there was no easier way to disarm me, than by affecting my breathing. This beast was reading me and attacking where it knew it would cause the greatest damage. I reached for my inhaler, slowly and calmly used it several times, never once taking my concentration off finding this thing. Realising its efforts had failed, it moved onto its next trick. In seconds the room became really dense. We couldn't really see each other, we were being separated and divided, and at the same time all experiencing different sensations. Patrick began to feel overwhelmed by the situation. Kevin was starting to feel angry. Lyn was having difficulty tuning in to what was happening. It was as if she was being battered with information. She could feel lots of other people present, so could Kevin; grandparents, great grandparents etc., this demon was using anyone and anything it could to distract from itself. I doubted the grandparents were really here. It was as if it was synthesising the whole event. Drawing on knowledge from both David and Hannah and using if for his own purposes. You could feel Hannah's anxiety when we talked about her recently departed granddad, a man she loved very much. Now she was getting fearful this demon would take her grandfather away. Or was her grandfather the demon? Where did one begin and the other end? You could feel her anxiety building up. We were beginning to have an impact on this demon, and it was going to throw everything it could at us. Without stopping what we were doing or losing concentration, I placed a reassuring hand on her arm. 'It's not your granddad,' I assured her. 'He is safe, it's the demon, pretending.' I smiled, she looked at me and in an instant I knew she trusted me. I explained to the group what it was doing. The bombardment stopped. Then came the smell. Sewage, gut-wrenching smells, began to seep into the room, it was as if you could taste it, almost see it, as the room began to darken. I had had enough now. It was time. I nodded to all the others, we began to power up, bringing the Guides as close as we could, so they could work through us. Reading my mind, a mass began to rise on the bed, like a living rock, it rose. You could feel its mighty power, but it was no match for four Guides and all the power of the Light. We began to blast it, wave after wave after wave came through us, as this beast was broken down. Slowly it began to shrink in size, as it began to cave in under the force of the light. In a few minutes it was reduced to nothing. We opened a doorway and threw it through, before it had chance to regain its power. Again, we had a building placed on some holy ground, an area where energy free flowed between the different dimensions. This property had trapped the freedom of movement and allowed this dark entity to bridge over into our world. At the same time, it had captured this visiting 'troll like creature'. Something from another dimension, a different world to ours. It had transversed here and was held captive by this darkness which had blocked the entrance back to its world. The vortex in the hallway. Somehow this darkness had found a way here and taken charge of the vortex. Using it for its own means. Bringing things in and trapping them here.

All the time we were at the property, I was drawn to the slope that led from the front of the house. I knew this was an energy line. There was another portal down the bank. I also knew we needed to build a wall of light, if we were to stop this thing from re-entering into their world, and possibly other things too. I couldn't see anything, but I was entranced by it. I tuned in. White Feather confirmed my suspicions. We were on ancient sacred ground, and we needed to sever the link between the two portals. This we duly did. By building up walls of silver light, layer after layer. We then diverted the energy line to the side of the house, so it could continue to flow, but away from this property.

We sealed the bungalow. We filled the house with light, and at the same time the smell of roses, brought by Hannah's granddad filled the property. Here was his confirmation, he was safe. He was nothing to do with the darkness. We gave Hannah a few messages from him. Her eyes filled with tears, she knew it was him and she knew he was safe. That is all the reassurance she needed.

I Can See You

The majority of the clearances have usually been filtered through me. Not on this occasion as the family were a friend of Dean's and I trusted Dean. If he told me there was a problem, then I believed him. Chris had been communicating with Dean over a couple of months. Caitlin had begun to experience nightmares, always the same about a shadow thing coming out of the floor and trying to drag her down a hole. She was becoming more distressed by this, and bedtime was beginning to turn into a nightmare. This only appeared to be bothering her not the little boy.

Chris had been a former work colleague. Over time Chris and his wife Michelle had become good friends. As the children — Caitlin and Freddie — came along the friendship had turned more to visits to the house than trips out and Dean had become quite fond of the children. Caitlin was six years old and Freddie two and a half. They had been in the current house for ten months and Caitlin was becoming increasingly distressed around bedtime and during the night. Dean had offered our services and off we traipsed to the far side of Stafford.

All communication had been done through text messages and the parents had been very careful not to mention our pending arrival. There was no one to look after the children and I was keen to speak to Caitlin. I was convinced by what Dean had told me that something else was going on and I was determined to try and discover what was troubling this child.

As we parked around the corner Dean received a text from Chris. He was really freaked out. Caitlin has asked Chris to ask Dean and his friends not to come. How did she know? Dean managed to persuade Chris for the evening to go ahead. The journey had probably swayed him, as they realised we had travelled quite a distance to get here.

After the introductions, Caitlin who normally loved Dean, refused to even look at him, instead clinging to her mother. Everyone else went upstairs and I tried to talk to Caitlin; I knew she held the key to what was troubling her. The family had not witnessed anything significant, but Caitlin was really troubled. As much as I tried to engage her in conversation, I was getting nowhere. Finally, I asked Caitlin if the man frightened her. She sat up and looked directly at me and asked if I could see him. I explained I could see what she could see. I enquired if he had told her not to talk to me. Her eyes shot around the room and she slowly nodded. I knew I needed to leave her out of this. She was so afraid of what was here we would have to carry on alone, so I thought.

Freddie's speech we were told was quite poor, and apart from the odd word he had not fully developed his speech to a level of communication where it was easy to understand the meaning, instead he spoke in 'baby talk', with Caitlin being his voice, which is probably why he was not progressing with his speech. As I walked to the stairs, I was shocked to see Freddie, walking quickly down the stairs with his arms folded firmly in front of him like a miniature Cossack dancer. I was terrified he would fall, but this little boy marched with such determination it was unbelievable. It was as if his sister had fallen by the wayside, but he was determined to drive this out of the house. He had never mentioned this beast to his family, but it was quite obvious he was very aware of this. He saw us and the option to get rid of this, and he was taking no chances.

His arms stayed in this position until the clearance was over, never moving, never faltering. The solar plexus is our centre of power. It is often thought that disembodied entities attack this zone in search of psychic food. How this little boy understood this I will never know, but it was certainly apparent he did. In fact, Freddie amazed most of us for the forty-five minutes it took us to sort out the problem. No matter how many times Chris took him downstairs, he was back in a shot. In the end we decided to let him stay. I think we were more concerned as he Cossacked up and down those stairs that he would fall.

We stood on the landing of the spacious house, so well presented, with its soft colours and immaculate thick beige carpets, but we were not convinced by the material side of this house. It has a foreboding feeling, the atmosphere felt charged, a sense as if something so very wrong was about to unfold in front of our eyes. We were all in agreement — we felt drawn to Caitlin's room. It was a beautiful room, a little girl's dream. Soft pinks and expensive furniture, tastefully decorated with images of snow white blended into the décor. Yet something was not right in this room. It was cold, dark, and just being in the room made the hairs stand up on your neck. The most sinister part of the room appeared to be where the elevated expensive pine bed stood, with a play area underneath, consisting of a desk and a little chair. Lyn and I nodded in agreement, the space on the underside of this bed was not good. As we exchanged comments and looks, in burst our little Cossack, who unfolded his arms briefly to point to the corner of the underside. He then flipped a light switch and soft little fairy lights lit up this space and the edge of Caitlin's bed. Chris was startled that Freddie even knew the location of the plug, which was well hidden behind the desk. Chris explained that Caitlin really did not like this space and they had recently fitted these lights to try and make it more inviting. In fact, she would not go to bed without the lights being put on first. Chris was now more perturbed about ensuring Freddie couldn't reach them in future.

Before any clearance we energetically seal the property. It is always an unfair battle as we work against something we cannot find with our five senses; this act gives us an advantage, as whatever is here is trapped and remains within the confines of the property until we have dealt with it.

Within a moment the tension in the rooms had gone. We all knew whatever was here had moved from this room. This was a shapeshifter. We tracked in down to the parents' room. There stood a huge black figure, standing in a poorly lit corner of the room. It pulsated a dark foreboding energy which appeared to electrically charge the room, almost challenging us to dare move closer. Chris began to feel increasingly uncomfortable. Bewildered, he was struggling to understand what was happening in the room. Dean, Lyn and I exchanged glances and a few well-placed nods, then we began to move into action, while trying to soothe Chris at the same time. In a moment it was gone. The room became calmer and lighter. Before we had a chance to speak, the little boy pointed underneath the bed and crouched down, then unfolded his arms and grew tall with his arms above his head. With a grimacing face, he growled and began to move across the room. I asked whether the was nasty man hiding underneath the bed. He nodded, then pulled me towards the bathroom and pointed to the underside of the bath, smiling and nodding. Does he hide here as well? He nodded his head frantically, with his arms back in their folded position. As we stood on the landing there was a clear breeze across this spacious area. We could all feel it, it was almost like standing on a small outcrop with the wind gently cleansing the area. As strange as it sounds, the area felt wet. Chris told us of water leaks where there was no source, wet patches on the floor and the ceiling above, but they could never find the source.

What Freddie couldn't tell us was where this had come from. If we were to win this battle, we needed to understand how this had got here, this would give us an idea of what we were battling with. Lyn was convinced this was a vortex, but not a natural one. Both Dean and I sensed mining underneath the ground. I was not familiar with this area but felt there had been mining here. Chris confirmed this. I had a sense this entity was not alone and was coming through a tunnel. I walked towards the window and there sat a strange cat, meowing loudly and looking directly up at me. This was it. 'Do you know of any mine shafts in the area?' I asked. There was one in the garden. Chris walked over, the cat had mysteriously disappeared, and Chris pointed to the exact spot. This was directly aligned through Caitlin's bedroom, cutting underneath her bed. This all began to make sense. I knew if we sealed this, we could stop further disturbances by blocking their entrances. We started by sealing both these holes.

We now had it trapped. We began to scan the upstairs to find it. Freddie completely understood what we were doing. He grabbed my arms and pulled me back into his parents' room and pointed to the underside of the bed. We placed Chris and Freddie in a protective bubble and began to manipulate the room size in order to flush out this entity. All we could see was a shape the size of a small spider, hiding in the corner. As we flushed it out, it sensed its doom, in a second it exploded into an angry aggressive entity at least six feet tall with an imposing energy towering above us, pushing and suppressing us. It was difficult to breath. We knew if we lost, this beast would be more powerful than ever. A five-minute psychic battle ensued, as we pitched against this angry evil entity. Supported by the other side, we manoeuvred this entity into a tube of energy and flushed it out of the house. We quickly sealed the house, ensuring there was no return. Little Freddie, held close in his daddy's arms, clapped his hands with joy.

We cleansed the energy from every room and went downstairs. Little Freddie unfolded his arms and walked down the stairs holding the handrail. As we entered the room Caitlin said, 'It's gone now, hasn't it?'

'Yes, forever,' I replied, and it is not coming back Lyn added.

Little Freddie acted as if nothing had happened, and as he would normally do, he went and got a book and climbed on Dean's knee to be read a favourite story.

Afterwards Caitlin told her mother a horrible man had told her to stop us coming as her mommy would be injured. She had been terrified by this. Chris and Michelle had been renting with the view to buy after a rather complicated sale of another house went through. They decided against this despite the money they had spent. It turned out they were not the only ones to experience problems, the last two tenants had turned out to be short-term lets, both cut short, both with young children who suffered from nightmares.

De-Cluttering the Ghost

Barbara lived with her grandson and granddaughter, both in their late teens, in a 1930s style semi-detached house. While she was separated from John, her husband, he was very supportive and visited several times a week. It was John who had found me. We had met years ago at a local Spiritualist Church, and he had remembered my interest in the paranormal. We readily agreed to help them. The problem was poltergeist activity, and most of it was around the children in their bedrooms. Clocks without batteries in would tick and alarm at obscure times. Lightbulbs would fall out and explode. Items would be thrown, moved, including a wash basket which was frequently upturned.

A lot of attention was focused on the grandson, who was being tormented at night. As soon as he turned off his light, the problems would start. He could sense a figure leaning over him, he thought he could smell their rancid breath and almost hear it. It would terrify him. From nowhere it would rush across the room at him, to the point where now he was afraid to turn off his bedroom light. It frequently woke him up with tapping and scratching sounds.

The granddaughter did not suffer nearly as much as the boy, but she complained of feeling someone was standing watching her when she was in the shower, to the point where she began to feel uncomfortable with having a shower in the house.

Barbara was a hoarder. The house was crammed with china dolls, dollhouses and pictures. When there was physically no wall space left to hang them, they sat on the floor, lining hallways, stairs and bedrooms. Ornaments covered every piece of furniture, and when there was no space left, they were placed on the floor. It was difficult to move around the house.

As stated previously, a lot of the activity was around the grandchildren, Millie, fourteen years old and Kyle, sixteen. Both were very intuitive and psychically gifted. Unfortunately, people with this type of gift shine a brighter light. Like moths to a light bulb, entities are attracted to this light. This is why gifted people are sometimes more prone to have this type of activity around them than other people.

When we are frightened, we give off bolts of energy. So we have brighter lights giving off greater power. To disembodied entities, human energy is power. If the entity can evoke fear in a human, they can use this to build up their power and to become more effective in our world. So you can see why entities may be attracted to people shining a brighter light.

Often a haunting will start off as just small things and increase over time. The activity increases because the entity has grown strong through the fear it has evoked. What started off with the occasional disturbance turns into a full-blown haunting.

We felt that that was what had happened here over time. Whatever was present here had grown more powerful.

As stated previously, all the rooms were crammed with furniture, pictures, dolls and ornaments, making it difficult to actually get in the rooms. The clutter will also make it more difficult to cleanse, as we are unable to reach the extremities and corners of the house.

We focused our attention on the bedrooms of the two children, where the main activity was occurring. As always, it is important to discover how the entity has entered into the house, to ensure we can close the portal and stop it from simply walking back in, after we had banished it. On this occasion there did not appear to be a route in, our search was proving futile. That was until we entered Kyle's bedroom. It was impossible to understand how he had managed to sleep in this room. The room was dank, dark and cold. Instead of feeling the warm relaxing ambience normally associated with a bedroom, there was a sense of everything being incredibly dirty, as if you would catch something if you touched it. Yet physically it wasn't dirty, just cluttered. We all felt very uncomfortable with the space and were quite eager to get out of the room.

As soon as we began to tune in, you could feel the energy of a very angry ghost which began to manifest itself, making its presence known. Individually the four of us tuned in and located 'it' in the corner of the room. Lyn had got its height at around five feet six inches, and we all agreed. This angry being was female. Using our psychic abilities, we were able to create an image of her. By using more than one medium, with each of us at this stage working independently, we are able to clarify what we can see. This stops the entity from trying to fool us, pretending to be something it isn't. Her clothes were Victorian. She wore a dark skirt, light-coloured blouse and her hair in a bun. Shaune pointed to the picture which lay on the bed. Oh, my goodness, it was the same woman. This entity was attached to her belongings. She was very angry her picture was in this house and she wanted it returned, now! It was right, this was a picture of her. It was difficult to understand how she had become attached to this picture, but she had, and she was so angry. The picture had been purchased from an antique shop. They in turn had purchased it from a car boot sale. I could not help but think silently, no wonder it was for sale.

We were unable to ascertain why or how this entity had become attached to this picture. She was so angry, she refused to communicate with us. Her bitterness had darkened her soul, she appeared ugly, very different from the image in the picture. It was impossible to reason with her, to help her to understand she was now dead and needed to go home. Every time I tried to communicate this with her, she became angrier than before, if possible, but she did.

She was determined she was going nowhere; and we were equally determined that she was. In the end she was removed to her proper world, kicking and screaming. The 'other side' would nurture her soul back to health, though healing.

Eventually, we managed to push her through the grey gateway we had created. I would have loved to send her higher, through a lighter doorway, but feared the light would blind her.

Moving her over was easier than clearing the dark energy which tainted every corner of the house. Before we left, we spent some time explaining to Barbara the issues an over-cluttered zone causes in terms of trapping stagnant energy, which in turn is liable to attract dark energies to her home.

As we sat in our debrief session in the pub, reflecting and cleansing ourselves, I was not convinced Barbara would heed our words, and suspected she would carry on as before, and before long would find herself in a similar situation.

Demons from Hell

I was not the first person or first choice for Amber. In fact, several people had already visited the property, including a local paranormal investigation organisation. During their visit, a cord from the blinds had wrapped around Amber's neck. During the night of their visit, very little activity was actually recorded. The medium that had accompanied the group had told her that she had a Demon alongside her. With very little evidence gained, they had merely gone away and left the situation as it was. Amber now had to face the wrath this of Demon who was angered that she had tried to get rid of it.

Paranormal investigation groups seek to gain evidence and information that paranormal activity is taking place. However, they do not offer solutions to the person or persons tormented by such activity. So they are of little or no practical use to the victims. They just anger the disembodied spirit.

By the time Lyn, Kevin, Patrick and I visited the property, Amber had lived with this torment for over seven years. In that time, she had moved properties numerous times, and each time the darkness merely followed her. Amber was at a loss to understand where this had come from, she had wracked her brains time and time again, trying to find the source, the starting point when it all began. Each time she drew a blank.

I spoke to Amber on the 'phone for a significant length of time prior to arranging to go and visit. During our conversation, she explained some of the paranormal activity which she had been subjected to; the list was endless. From almost as soon as her daughter could talk, the Demon began to talk to her. On one occasion warning her she was in real trouble, as the demon was really angry with her. Amber was too shocked to ask her what she meant. Her daughter had three names for this entity — Kesdeja, Charlie and Tema, and it was clear from the conversations Amber had with her daughter that this Demon or Demons were conversing with her daughter on a regular basis. Amber had been sexually assaulted on a regular basis, including an attempt to have penetrative sex, and something regularly coming behind her and grasping her breasts. She had been tormented by swarms of flies and wasps. Books had been stacked on top of each other to towers of up to four feet in height; in fact, anything that could be stacked was being stacked in all of the houses she lived in. Her bedding was folded into perfect triangles and every cupboard door was opening in seconds. She had been pushed down the stairs on numerous occasions: doors slamming all over the house was a regular occurrence. On a regular basis she had had contact with this entity during her sleep state, often when she was falling

77

asleep, immediately it would enter into her dreams. She would wake up terrified yet was unable to get out of her bed. She had on several occasions rung her mother in the middle of the night, hysterical, telling her of the fear she felt. Her sceptical partner had, however, witnessed a huge shadow rising out of the floor and slowly moving across the room. Despite his own reserve, even he on this occasion could not deny what he had just witnessed. On another occasion, he had choked on a tiny tablet, reporting that he felt like it was stuck in his throat. Pet after pet had died from the strangest of conditions. But the final act that had driven her to seek further help was when the contents of a hot cup of tea somehow shot out of her husband's mug and landed all over the baby, resulting in hospitalisation. It was this final act which had sent her in search of help through the internet: and she had found me and my friends. Due to diary commitments, it almost seemed as if it was going to take us an age to get here. So some careful shifting of diaries meant we were able to visit very quickly.

Lyn, Kevin, Patrick and I arrived at this elegant modern three-storey house, which had been carefully designed to fit in with the older properties in this small village. From the outside, it looked beautiful, but it felt anything other than this. You could feel the vibration instantly on entering, and it felt anything other than comfortable.

We made our way into the lounge, where we sat and spoke to Amber for several minutes, as we tried to ascertain precisely what the problem was that we were facing here. Amber did not look well, she had dark circles underneath the eyes, and dark patches within her auric field. What she told us was clear, that somehow this entity had become entangled in her own energy field, and wherever she went it followed her. While husband, daughter and the baby had been subjected to contact and attacks from this entity, it was clear that in the main it was focused on Amber.

I also knew that we would not be able to deal with this in one night. This was going to require at least one more visit, if not another on top of that. Often, when there is a powerful dark energy, it will capture within its own energy field numerous other entities, or lost souls. It will hold them captive for his own gratification, forcing them to carry out evil deeds with the desired outcome that fear is created. Fear is the food of darkness. Fear converts into power. The more fear that can be conjured up, the greater the power the entity will have. Therefore, if it has several others working on its behalf, it is able to generate large amounts of fear, which will in turn be converted to power. In their own world, these entities are extremely powerful. In our world, it takes time for them to be able to collect and create the power, which will replicate their power in their own world. Therefore, the longer they go on undetected, and terrify anyone who comes into their pathway, the stronger they become. These entities have huge power surge capabilities. They live in the psychic world, but as they build their power, they are able to operate within the physical world and can physically move objects and conjure vile smells and swarms of insects. As we worked with Amber, we soon realised the extent of these entities' power and exactly how many people were held captive by this Demon. This was further complicated by Amber's moving into a property which sat on a very powerful ley line, right across a vortex. This was a disaster waiting to happen

It was difficult to know where to begin. The group began by walking round the room and sensing the energies and vibrations in the lounge and kitchen. All were drawn to a corner on an adjoining wall. This really shocked Amber. She went on to show us a picture she had taken several days before. She had randomly taken a picture of the external wall, looking out on to the street by the window. In the middle of the two windows was a mirror, and in the mirror a figure could clearly be seen, the outline of the head and shoulders, this was a reflection of the corner in question.

We began to focus our attentions on and around Amber herself. I asked each and every one of the group, how many spirits they felt were involved. Everyone was in agreement, they felt that there were three. Kevin went one stage farther and began to detail the heights of the three entities he could picture around Amber. 'One is about three feet tall, another is of average height and the third one is massive,' he said. The other two nodded in agreement. For me he had described precisely what I could see. To the right of Amber, entwined with her aura, were three entities, all packed in close together. The only variation was that the tallest of the three was just a black outline, there appeared to be no real substance to it. When we mentioned the smaller of the three, Amber went on to tell us she had seen a small figure scurrying across her bedroom and had assumed it was her daughter. But when she leapt out of bed, her daughter was fast asleep. The little one was like a gnome or an elf, and definitely was not of this world.

Later we were to discover that Amber had used a Ouija board on numerous occasions. This answered all our questions. There was the source, a rip in the ether and the doorway through to the second dimension. Yet while the thing was the size of gnome, it was white in colour, extremely white. Its face was a ghastly white colour, with huge round staring eyes. On its head was a tall hat with a brim. He was going to be the first focus of our attention. Together we held the vibration and using our guides to lead us and show us, we pulled him from the grasp of the large black outline. It seemed the correct way on this occasion was to remove those that were held captive by the shadow. He gave very little resistance to our efforts to send him back, a clear indication that we were dealing with something that was being held against its will. Next, we concentrated on the man, a figure of normal height. Again, while it took immense effort to break it free from her energy field and away from the shadow, once we had got it free, it seemed to glide through the window back to the other side.

Next, we began to focus on the shadow. In a moment it was gone. I was not convinced we had managed to push it through the door, I felt it had gone into hiding. The property was sealed, so it was going nowhere, we began to search and search while I casually spoke to Amber about the evening. Mentally we swept each room, looking in every corner and cranny through-out the house, we would not stop until we had found what we were looking for. Suddenly I became aware of a figure to her right. At the same time, Amber asked, if it was possible she had known this thing, or had some connections to it, as it seemed to know her inner thoughts. As I looked at her, I could see her dad to her left and a great grandmother; I knew these had been trying to protect her, to lessen the effect of their presence. While they were not powerful enough to stop it all together, they could certainly cover her in love. I also became aware of a big powerful figure and I wrongly assumed this was the dark shadow. 'Do you have an ex-boyfriend who is in the spirit world,' I asked.

'Yes, I do,' she answered steadily, holding my gaze.

'Do you want him to go?' I asked.

'No,' she said. 'I want answers.'

'Amber, you have to ask him to go, otherwise I cannot force him to leave you.'

'I need answers,' she added.

I didn't feel I could talk to this entity, it didn't feel safe. 'Ask him to go,' I said again.

'Yes, go,' she said very hesitantly. As she said it, I felt something jump from her aura and psychically hit me. We began to push it through the doorway, back to the 'other side'. I was not convinced we had entirely won the battle, yet we still soldiered on and on, pushing him through the other side.

Before we left, we filled the house with light, we replaced the dark dank energy of the lounge, kitchen and bedroom. Convinced we had done as much as we could, be said our goodbyes. I told Amber to contact me if she felt or saw anything untoward. I added that often we cannot capture it in one go, several visits were required until we had freed the property of all its unwelcome occupants.

As we sat together in the pub reflecting the evening, we were all in agreement, we would be back. Amber's reluctance to release the ex-boyfriend would be the doorway back in for it. It was only going to be a matter of time before it was back in the house. I don't think any of us were ready for the speed in which it did re-appear!

The next day I had a call from Amber and she explained after we had left, she had gone up to bed, when the light fitting in her bedroom began to swing, and so did the one in her daughter's bedroom and the one on the landing. Simultaneously all the light fittings were swinging wildly from side to side. Amber went to go downstairs as soon as she placed a foot on the first step, she felt a force from behind pull her head and shoulders back and she fell down the stairs. Evidence of this could be seen on her knees, ankle and thighs, which were black and blue with bruises. I was not expecting it to come back quite so soon. Together we came up with a time to return the following night. This had to be squeezed in around a lot of other things.

Both Kevin and Patrick had quite a distance to come. So I decided, as there was only a little of the dark energy left, Lyn and I could do this ourselves. I made my mind up. I went to my laptop and tried to turn it on. The screen was completely blank, just like a few weeks previously. I would need the services of Patrick, an adept computer repair person. I stopped suddenly in my tracks. Immediately I knew this was a warning for me, this was too much for Lyn and I to do on our own, we needed a team at full strength. This was not going to be removing a lost soul, but something far more sinister. I took the computer breakdown as a warning and called both Kevin and Patrick to help Lyn and I. This was a decision I would not regret.

Apart from the swinging lampshades and the fall on the stairs, there had been no further activity. Liam, Amber's husband, was about. He was upstairs with the baby in their bedroom. It was clear going upstairs was not an option. Yet I was adamant, we needed to go into the bedrooms and check out the upper floor. Nothing could sway me from that, I knew we would find the problem on the upper floor. After a while we swapped places with Liam the husband. He came downstairs into the lounge and we went into their bedroom. As soon as we walked into the room, I knew we had found the source. The main light was off and the room was lit by the light from the en suite bathroom. The room was dark and foreboding; Lyn and Patrick immediately pointed to the left of the double bed, by the window. This was where Amber slept. While we searched, walked and talked, Amber sat on the bed, on her half. There was the ex-boyfriend. As I began to tune in, Amber told me there was something else. As she had begun to fall asleep on the Saturday night, she had heard two voices talking together simultaneously, one was high pitched, the other low, yet as they spoke, they said the same words to her. 'She would never be rid of them unless I could figure out their reason for being there.' No pressure then I thought, so I began talking to this dark figure by the side of the bed. Here we had the ex-boyfriend back again. I was determined not to push him over until I had established what was wrong, what was keeping him here. I was standing to the left of the bed, Lyn to the right; Kevin was closer to me, and Patrick to Lyn, both were positioned at the foot of the bed. I began to open a link with him.

'Amber, this man died very, very quickly.' I banged my hands together to show an impact.

'Yes, he did,' she said.

'He died at the scene and there was nothing anyone could have done to help him,' I added.

'That's so true, he was decapitated,' she said.

'He loved you very much, but your father did not approve, in fact he was closer to your father's age than yours.'

'True.' She nodded.

'Dad did not approve of his little girl being involved with this man,' I said. She nodded her head in agreement. I went on to add, despite the age difference he loved her very much. Amber then informed us he had been found with an engagement ring on him at the point of death. 'You know this ring was for you, don't you,' I added. She nodded her head. I also went on to tell her people had said some terrible, terrible things about him after he died. He was clearly upset and he wanted her to know that they were all untrue. People were tarnishing his name for no reason. I again repeated to her they were all falsehoods and asked her whether she understood this. I implored her as I knew this man would never leave until he had got across to her that he was not really a bad man. You could see the truth spread across her face; yes, she did believe him. I felt his energy change, he would now be willing to go.

As this began to draw to the end, I became aware of Kevin. His face was bright red and he was clearly distracted by something. He began to take off his coat. I turned and looked at him and he said, 'There is something else in this room and it is pure evil, I can feel it, it is really bothering me, I can't breathe properly, it's up there. It has come in on the back of this man's anger.'

As he spoke Kevin gestured towards the ceiling. I asked him to focus on this entity while we dealt with the ex.

Lyn turned to me and said, 'He is ready to go now, look he has turned his back on us and is now facing the wall.' There was no need to call in loved ones or Guides to help in the final transition, he had said what he wanted to say and now he was ready to go and meet his maker. So Kevin focused on the ceiling while the rest of us facilitated this entity's exit from our world. He went peacefully, he had made his peace and now he was ready to go. We all felt him leave. I explained to Amber what had happened. As I spoke, I saw a dark shadow, which for all intents and purposes was the shape of a female womb, float across the adjoining wall. With intent it slowly left the spot where the ex had been, and had moved along the one wall onto the other, precisely where Kevin had been focusing his attention. All three reported they too could see it and tracked it as it traversed across the two walls.

'Oh, my goodness, I can see it too, I really can,' added Amber. It merged with the dark spot Kevin had so carefully watched. This was really difficult to understand what was going on here. This was a living intelligence, yet it appeared to be made up of several things. More than one entity resided within the black mass, so did the tortured souls of several animals, entwined with the shadow of darkness. I looked again at Kevin, his face was blood red and there were dark patches forming on his head, as it wrapped itself around

87

him. I turned to Lyn, she was also showing signs that the entity had penetrated her aura. She had big dark circles underneath her eyes and her skin was as white as could be. I looked from Kevin to Lyn, it was attacking fifty percent of the team at one time. This was an incredibly powerful entity we had here, to penetrate two together and not be in fear of being overcome. It felt it was a match for all four of us and our Guides. I knew this was a true Demon we were dealing with.

'Deal with Kevin first, I will hold it here,' Lyn said, so that is precisely what we did, we pulled it off Kevin first. You could feel Kevin using every ounce of energy to keep this Demon in check and stopping it from controlling him. Kevin is a big powerful guy, if he had lost control, none of us, even working together, would have managed Kevin, who is six feet tall and at least sixteen stones, most of which is muscle. For several minutes a battle ensued, and we ripped the Demon, breaking its hold on him. At the same time, Kevin fought from within, exerting his own power over this evil, intelligent mass. Finally, we had removed it. Kevin's complexion went from bright, angry red to normal, all black blots were gone.

We now turned our attention to Lyn. I had to know why it was here if I was to get rid of it. We moved Lyn to where Kevin had stood, and I began to watch her and see what was happening. I felt its tentacles move closer to her and wrap themselves around as it gained a bigger hold. She too began to turn into a violent shade of red, with dark patches forming all over her body as it began to blend into her energy.

'Why are you here?' I asked.

'Because I can,' she spat.

Not good enough, I thought. 'Why are you here, answer me,' I demanded.

'Because I can,' she repeated. The voice was deep and broken and the words were spat, this sounded like nothing I had ever heard before.

'Not good enough, answer me,' I almost screamed. At this point she flew at me, her fists raised, she seriously meant me some harm. Kevin was having none of it, her pushed her back, pinning her against the door, trapping her legs from kicking out at either of us. 'Answer me,' I repeated.

'Two Girls.'

I had heard enough, I knew it was the Ouija board. When it was least expecting it, I hit Lyn with a huge bolt of energy conjured up from myself and powered by the other side. As it hit Lyn she fell to the ground. She seemed to go down in a dead faint. We were to find out later as it hit her with the energy it exited from the top of her head, knocking her to the floor. It was now loose and shooting round the room, we had to capture it and deal with it. It shot directly into the attic. Fortunately for us, the ladders for the loft were down and we were able to follow it up and send it on its way. What was interesting was at the point when Lyn collapsed, Amber said she felt about a stone lighter, as if a huge weight had been pulled off her. She kept repeating how weird it was.

We moved around the house from room to room searching any signs or strands of energy from this Demon, carefully planted so it could return back in the future. We looked everywhere but couldn't find anything. The final room we went into was the playroom on the lower ground floor. The energy in here was terrible.

'We cannot get this place warm,' Amber told us. The energy was awful. I could sense an air-raid shelter fear from the war. Orbs constantly flew around the room.

'Did you see those orbs?' Patrick asked. Yes, we all replied. They were flying everywhere.

'I can see animals being slaughtered,' Kevin said. He then asked Amber if she knew of anything like this round this area. She didn't.

This is what had helped to power this Demon, the house stood close to or on a major ley line. This line held both the negative and positive vibrations of the area. Unfortunately, in this case, it was the negative vibrations it feasted upon. Eons of negativity were held around this area, and it had used it for its own good. We were to discover later that indeed a slaughterhouse had resided very close to this area. We spent an age cleansing out this room of years and years of darkness which had stagnated in this area. No doubt more had been pulled in by this Demon, almost like a pantry to feast on at its will. We then attempted to shift the line as far away from the property as we could. We then replaced it with more vibrant energy.

Exhausted, we said our goodbyes, confident that it was going to be a while before we would return, if ever. I felt sure we had done all we could here, and there were no signs of it left. In fact, there was more attached to us, than left in the property.

We sat in the pub as we checked each and every one of us out for shards of energy, implants, attachments, etcetera. As we reflected, Kevin spoke of the blind anger he had felt and how it had taken everything he had to fight it off. He described it as a black mass slowly trying to overtake him, to provoke him to hurt and hit out. Lyn shared his sentiments with him. We realised the animals caught up in the black mass were from the slaughterhouse, from years ago; he had found a way of either evoking their souls back here or awakening something. Whatever the black mass had done, he had managed to bring in a whole array of lost souls, darkness, trapped souls, etcetera. He had then held them captive and used them for his own will. This was not some lost soul, here you had a Demon and a very powerful and intelligent Demon who knew precisely what he was doing. The longer he stayed, the more powerful he got.

I was to find out later that the daughter knew its name, she called him Kasdeja, Assim, Charlie and Tema. I was able to research Kasdeja, who is referred to in the book of Enoch as a fallen angel, who is described as the fifth Satan. A translation of the books said:

'...And the fifth was named Kasdeja: this is he who showed the children of men all the wicked smitings of spirits and demons, and the smitings of the embryo in the womb.'

That we saw the shape of this entity travelling across the wall and it looked like a womb is no surprise.

Do you Know this Ghost?

I had known Eddie for years. I had initially met her
when I was manager of a home for older people. Over
the next fifteen years, periodically our paths would
cross. Eddie made contact with me after my first book
was published. She later joined my development circles
and developed into a proficient medium. After a couple
of years of turbulence and unsettlement, Eddie finally
found a house that was to be home for her and her son,
Josh, who was a truly gifted child. Unfortunately, all
was not to be well in the house, and within weeks of
moving in, Josh began to see things and sense that
someone was talking to him and telling him to do
horrible things to both his mother and his father.

Eddie was in a real dilemma. She didn't feel
anything untoward in the house, yet on the other hand,
she knew that things were not right and that something
was clearly disturbing Josh. What made Eddie think that
there was something untoward was that the baby next
door screamed incessantly. Eddie felt the baby was
being tormented by something. She herself had tried to
tune in and find out what was going on, but she felt she
was too close to the situation and unable to conclude one
way or the other. Eddie had been on several clearances

with me. She knew the power of darkness and every instinct told that this baby was being tormented by some unseen force. As soon as Eddie told me the story, I felt she was right and volunteered almost immediately to go to the house and talk to Josh to try and ascertain if the problem was indeed an unearthly influence. I didn't feel we needed a whole team in order to address these issues, and in fact I felt even better if I didn't go in mob-handed, as this may have been too much for Josh.

So Lyn and I went, just the two of us. Josh was not expecting us and seemed quite surprised when we arrived. He shot an accusing glance across at his mom. In response Eddie said, 'Don't look at me, you asked me to get my spiritual friends to come and sort this problem out and here they are.' A look of recognition came across his face, he had indeed asked Eddie to bring her friends along to try and sort out the problem.

Lyn and I sat down and spent a few moments trying to put Josh at ease. I explained that we had come to check the house over and ensure that there was nothing untoward that was trying to communicate with him. And if there was, we would send them back where they belonged. All the time I was speaking, this clever, gifted boy watched and read and analysed me. After a few minutes, I pointedly said to Josh, 'Is there someone I can see talking to you?' He looked at me, searching my face, trying to decide what he thought I wanted to hear, weighing it against the truth. I could sense his dilemma 'Come on, Josh, you can tell me. You know you cannot

94

hide the truth from me, because I can see what you can see.' I looked carefully at Josh, and he looked back. He knew I could see the same as he could see. His gaze never left my face and slowly he began to nod his head. I asked again, 'Is there someone who keeps talking to you that no one else can see?' Josh began to relax, and this time nodded his head with a lot more vigour. I then added, 'Don't worry, because by the time I leave today, he will be gone, I shall help him go home to his own mom and dad and there he will be happy. I looked at Josh and waited for his response. I knew that Josh would have to be at ease and peace with what I was about to do. While this disembodied entity had been anything but nice to Josh, it was important that I had Josh on side with me. If I didn't, this entity would have a doorway back through. And the doorway would be Josh.

I then explained to Josh what Lyn and I were about to do, with the help of his mom. We were going to try to find out who it was that was disturbing him. With the thought in mind that we had a vulnerable twelve-year-old here, a lot was done with a nod and a glance. I would soon find out that our efforts to try to conceal and protect Josh from what we were doing were futile. He could see everything that was going on. Together we began to search and scan the house. I sensed that whatever it was, it was not in the property. It was next door. Lyn confirmed my thoughts. So we began to pull a wall of energy from the adjoining property through into Eddie's lounge. As we did, so we netted ourselves the ghost. I turned to Josh and said, 'Is there anybody in the room with us, Josh?' He looked at me and nodded. 'Where are they?' I asked. Without saying a word, he pointed towards the ceiling on the wall adjoining the two properties. This is precisely where it was, hanging, suspended in mid-air. I turned to Lyn and gave her a knowing glance, she nodded. She knew precisely what I was asking without any words being spoken. We had got him. A wall of silver energy had dragged this entity from its hiding place.

He was not a happy spirit. I began to describe how this man looked. I said that he was around 'five feet six inches tall, and not aged well. His face was lined and ravaged by time and his lifestyle, he was clearly a smoker and an alcoholic. He was extremely thin and a very angry man. He wasted no time in trying to verbally abuse me. As I spoke, Eddie stared at me. A look of recognition came across her face. 'It's Ken, Ken Jones! I know him!' Eddie went on to explain that when she was a manager working on the district, she had to visit the man next door to a client on numerous occasions because of this attitude towards staff. Yes, he did smoke, yes, he did drink, and yes, he was exactly the way that I had described him.

We knew what we had. We held him in a box of light. All that was left to do now was to send him on his way. I turned my energies back to this entity, now with true conviction. I could call the entity by his correct name. This time I spoke loudly, so Josh could hear what was going on. At the same time, I communicated telepathically, telling the spirit to go through the doorway or we would push him through. Either way, he was going to depart from this plane.

'Ken,' I called. 'Your mother is here. Can you see her? Turn around and look,' I said. 'Your mum is calling you, arms outstretched towards you.' She has always loved you and now wants you to join her.' Slowly Ken began to turn around and look at the opening we had created in the ether. And there stood his white-haired mother, beckoning Ken to come into her loving arms. We then began to send waves of encouraging energy and began pushing him to the other side. At one point he was not going and was clinging dearly to the edge of the doorway. I stopped and turned to Josh and said, 'What is he doing now, Josh?'

'He is holding onto the side, he doesn't want to go, I don't think,' Josh said.

'He does, he's just a little frightened at the moment, so we are going to give him a little bit of help,' I said.

I now felt this had gone on long enough. So Eddie, Lyn and I gave one almighty blast of energy as we pushed him through the doorway. And then we quickly sealed it. Moments later, Josh turned to me and said, 'He has gone now.' As he spoke, he nodded his head. Yes, indeed he was right. Ken was now back where he belonged.

When I saw Eddie the following week, she reported that things were now much better at home. What she found to be rather telling was that from that moment on, she never heard that baby scream again. Yes, of course she could still hear the baby crying, but nothing like that soul-piercing scream that she used to hear before, which used to last for up to an hour at a time. All was now well.

Frightening Children

Ben had been no stranger to paranormal activity. He had lived through it for most of his life, at his mother's house. And now it seemed to have followed him here to his first home of his own. Perhaps it was no coincidence, as when we looked on the map, his new home was positioned diagonally to his mother's house, sitting on the same ley line. Emma, Ben's partner, first contacted me through Facebook. Initially, nothing seemed too alarming and I didn't feel it was anything to worry about.

It was only when they described what it was doing to their little girl that I began to become concerned, and hastily gathered a team together. Emma and Ben had been in the house for six months. In truth, it had never felt right from the beginning. Both said the house was unwelcoming, and it didn't feel like how they thought it would feel, moving into their first home together. They had terrible problems with the drains, so they thought, but endless visits from the landlords and professionals could find nothing wrong, yet a putrid smell filled the house. Summer, the little girl, would point at her bedroom window and through the limited words of a two-year-old would say 'bad man'. Ben had woken in the night to see a dark shadow bending over him: the list was long. Probably the final straw for Emma was an incident with Summer. Emma was upstairs with the new baby and Summer. For a split second she took her eyes off Summer. Then she heard a scream. The little girl had somehow been lifted over the stair gate and transported downstairs and was now standing by the front door, with her coat on! All this had happened in seconds. While Summer seemed bothered by the experience, for Emma and Ben this was the last straw, and through his mother he contacted me.

On the night of our visit, confusion seemed to reign. Confusion about the time we were to start left Patrick sitting outside alone for thirty minutes. Trying to put the car in the shade for the dog was another misunderstanding. I knew it straight away, this thing was waiting for us. It was outside the property, trying to cause disharmony amongst us, before we had even gotten inside.

This thing meant business, but then again, so did we. So conscious of its desire, we joined together as one. It was eight o'clock on a hot summer's evening, and so warm that we were concerned about the dog in the car, yet as we entered this house, a wall of cold hit us. It seemed impossible that a house could be so cold on such a warm night.

Emma and Ben felt that the biggest problems were upstairs, in the bedrooms. However, there had been problems in almost every room in the house. You could see that this young couple had gone some way to try to make this house a home. Nice wallpaper with a bold pattern had been placed across one wall, and matching tones on the other three. They had several videos of the patterns on the walls spinning. Ben had been incredibly close to his nan, she had featured very much in his life. On one occasion he had come in the room to find a picture having moved several feet lying on the floor, yet the frame remained unbroken.

We were fascinated. You could look at the patterned wallpaper and see shimmer, and watch the patterns physically move. Yet there was no rational explanation, such as a heat source below.

Normally when we work, our focus is not on gaining evidence through photography or videos, we rely on what we sense and see, building up a full picture by communications with each other; never fully sharing the story, and waiting to see if others are drawn to the same part of the room as you are, or see the same things as you see, using their third eyes. This is the difference between ghost hunters and clearers: one is seeking to discover if there is something there, the others are there to find whatever is troubling the occupants and to get rid of it.

However, on this occasion we decided to take some footage. The orbs in the bedrooms were fascinating. While these are usually easy to see through the lens of a camera, on this occasion they were so powerful, you could actually see them with your eyes.

Ben was initially quite embarrassed to share his story, but now he was being driven by the desire to rid his family of whatever was tormenting them. He said that whenever he walked, he could see a dark shadow walking alongside him, this had been following him around now for over eighteen months. He produced a picture of an image he had captured through the rear mirror of his car. On reflection, I wished I had kept a copy of it, but on this occasion our focus was on dealing with whatever was tormenting this family. The picture was awful. A hag in black could clearly be seen on the back seat. Ben was convinced this was following him wherever he went.

We noted as we moved from room to room that there were no door handles on the doors. I couldn't help but ask why the door handles were missing. It turned out that on two occasions their daughter Summer had been locked in the bedroom and they were unable to open the door. As they had grown increasingly terrified, the door mysteriously just opened. Vowing never to be in this situation again, they had removed the catches on the doors from the three bedrooms upstairs.

The area where the property sat was steeped in a history of witchcraft, hauntings, and was believed to be set on some very powerful ley lines. There had been stories stretching back over time reporting sightings of soldiers long dead marching across the land.

It would seem that Ben and Emma had unfortunately rented a property sitting directly on this energy grid.

Without a doubt, the problem did appear to be centred on Ben. It was not that he was possessed, being controlled by this dark shadow. But somehow it had become entangled in his auric field. It was as if the entrapment was unintentional, but the dark shadow was unable to disengage from Ben's aura. Ben, on the other hand, did not know how to release what can best be described as a Hag. As with many Demons, they rarely come alone. They are often accompanied by lost souls whom they find walking the planet, who they then use for their own means. On this occasion, it would seem that the Hag had no lost soul in tow but had brought with it some smaller black shadows. These were about three feet in height, with piercing red eyes. The shapes were shifting from a semi-human form to black shadows, through to small black concentrated masses of energy.

We found these in both the bedroom of the little girl and Ben's room. We quickly gathered them together, and without communication or consultation, swiftly and deftly pushed them through a dark doorway back to whence they came.

However, the biggest battle was yet to come. And this was to disengage the shadow from Ben's aura. We needed his consent and assistance if we were to be successful. The difficulty is that when a Demon is so closely entangled with a human, it is very easy for them to influence the behaviour of that human. We could only admire Ben's determination to be rid of his black shadow.

There then followed twenty minutes of pushing, pulling, and cutting before we could finally confirm amongst ourselves and calmly say, 'It's gone.'

'I have just felt it leave me, I feel so light,' Ben said with a smile. Instantaneously, the room became warmer and lighter. You could physically feel and see the change in the atmosphere of the whole house.

Ben turned to me and told me he knew why Summer had not been upset or disturbed by some of the events that were occurring around her. He told me his nan had been there with her all the time, looking after her, keeping her safe. He went on to explain that at the moment of separation, his nan had appeared before him and told him that the Hag had been banished and would never bother him again. She had then given him reassurance that she had looked after his daughter during all these events and episodes over the last few months. It was almost as if Ben was a different man, and Emma also seemed renewed. It gave them such joy to know their daughter had indeed been protected and kept safe from these vile entities.

From the Caverns Below

Most people do not know what to do, or where to go, when troubled by the unseen and the unknown. This is probably why I had so many people come to me from Chrissie's shop in Dudley. This is how Richard and his family found me. As usual, they were at the end of their tether. Five years ago, they had bought their house, at a bargain price. Since then, the market had collapsed and they could see no way out of moving out. The list of difficulties was endless. The house was always dark. It smelt of rotting food and drains, and nothing seemed to solve the problem. The local Council had resorted to digging up the drains all around the property, but there was nothing wrong. The children refused to sleep in their own beds. At two, four and six this was proving to be quite a problem. They all suffered from nightmares. But rather eerily, the nightmares were the same for all of them. A monster would appear in the bedroom and growl at them. It would tower over them and try to eat them. When they separately described the monster, they each described the same. This really freaked out Richard's wife, Karen.

We arrived en masse on a summer's night. It was still very light outside, yet inside the house there was no light at all. The lounge light was permanently on, day and night. Yet it was still so dull in there. I could not believe how dull it was. I turned to Richard and said, 'It's not very bright in here, is it?'

I could see he hadn't really thought about it, because he just replied, 'It's always like this.'

Then we found it, here was the source. Well, here was part of it. It felt as if we had a dark column of energy reaching up from the ground and leading up into the bedroom. Before proceeding upstairs, I stood for a moment in the kitchen. The room was beautifully decorated, yet it felt ugly, as if the atmosphere was charged with something. The corner of the room appeared to drop away. In fact, the whole room gave the illusion that the bottom part of the kitchen was at least six inches lower than the top part. When you stood in the bottom, it felt like there was an echo, as if you were in a cavern. We were all drawn to the garden. You could feel a hole in the middle of the lawn. 'Do you know if there is mining underneath here, I asked?'

'Yeah, it's the limestone mines,' Richard replied. Yes, I could feel them, and that somehow the caverns were exerting influence on this house, including part of the garden. Perhaps the mining had caused this problem, who knows, but somehow, the ground had shifted. Interestingly enough, this was not the only house I had cleansed in this area. In fact, it was one of about ten, none of the occupants knowing about the others.

We began to walk up the stairs. I couldn't do it. A very strong force was pushing me down the stairs. So I held onto the rails and began to pull myself up, yet still it held me in abeyance. I could sense a darkness almost like a grey cloud, with a menacing face, which could appear and disappear in a moment. It could shift in size from a huge force, like it was now, shrinking down to a tiny black ball. Now it was the giant grey cloud, and it threw everything against me to stop me climbing the stairs. I tried. I could not gain enough strength to overcome it. As I pushed, so it pushed harder. Then a huge surge of power from this entity, knocked me backwards. As I began to fall backwards down the stairs, at the last moment I managed to steady myself, clinging onto the banister rail. I turned to Lyn and said, 'I can't climb the stairs, it won't let me. It's pushing me down.'

'Come on, I will help you,' she said.

So with Lyn pushing and me trying with all my might, I eventually managed to get to the top of the stairs. All the time Kevin had stood at the top of the stairs, looking in pure amazement. I was not expecting this at all. Here we had a living energy that could think, and it had planned its attack against us. I was mindful that we needed to be extremely careful if we were to overcome this thing. As quickly as it had reared up, so it shrunk back to the size of a tennis ball but remained equally as sinister. There was only one room it didn't seem to penetrate, that was a small box room. We all commented on this. Richard confirmed that this is precisely what the family felt. This was the only room where anyone felt safe. Kevin walked into the bathroom. He sensed a past hanging, as if a small female was hanging limply from the shower head. This didn't make sense. As he described her clothing, I could sense her, but her clothing didn't fit with the introduction of shower heads. Here we had another entity that had the ability to create whatever impression it wanted to give. Here it was firing us up, manipulating us with this young girl. I could see her dark, lank hair hanging around her shoulders, her thin, ragged body hanging limply from the shower, as if she had been murdered. We were being manipulated. As soon as I said that, it was gone, so was the awful presence in the shower room, a feeling so dark, it made you afraid to enter into the room.

We decided the room we needed to concentrate on was the parents' bedroom. The energy was awful. The room was extremely well decorated, yet it felt dirty, stale and dank. An awful smell filled the room, the energy was overwhelming, I really didn't want to stay in this room. I couldn't help myself. I turned to Richard and said, 'How have you managed to sleep in this? It's awful.'

'I know, but we have had no choice.'

I could have choked on my own words and my tactlessness here. The truth is they didn't have any choice at all did they? They were trapped here.

'Never mind, it will soon be gone,' I added, reassuringly.

We had it pinned in the room. The temperature began to change and so did Richard. 'I'm feeling really hot and uncomfortable,' he said. I tried to re-assure him it would be over soon. He nodded in agreement. So we began to try and force this thing into a corner so we could begin to do battle. As we did, we could see tentacles stretching from it to both Kevin and Richard. Kevin was adept at dealing with this and whatever it sent to him, he battled back. Richard was not. Suddenly he went for his throat.

'I can't breathe,' he gasped. We turned our attention to Richard. It went to escape, it could not; we held it, locked up the corner. Then part of itself broke away, like it could split into two. A black ball of energy scuttled around the room. Transversing the edge of the room, ducking under furniture for cover, it dashed from the room. It could not get far, the house was completely sealed, we would find it later. In the meantime, we fought to get the tentacles that were wrapped around Richard. Firstly, from his throat, then his stomach. He could hardly breathe as we plied concentrate energy rays at his throat. Slowly the grip was loosened, only to shoot another one directly into his solar plexus area. He writhed in pain as we again pulled and sliced to get it off. We removed the second one. Only slithers left but we didn't care, we would deal with those later. Now we concentrated on this small ball of power. Twice it reared up to over seven feet tall. It made no difference, we felt or saw no fear, just continued to do battle with it. Finally, we pushed it through the hole in the ether we had created. We spent ages trying to remove this room of the dank, dark vibrations. Slowly the light began to return and the horrendous smell faded. Finally, we found it hiding in the living room. The vibration in this room mirrored the bedroom. I bit my bottom lip and did not mention it. Lyn and I glanced at each other. We were both thinking the same. How did the family sit in this room, night after night? Fear filled the whole atmosphere. How had these three children lived in this? None of them would go to the toilet alone, or the shower or sleep alone. How must it have felt to exist in the shadow of this powered disembodied beast? We had it trapped and again it went for Richard. I wondered how much he could take in one night. At the same time, tentacles were thrown at both Lyn and I, but we were waiting. In moments we had cut them down, weakening it even more. Still, it clung onto Richard, this time attacking his heart. We all knew the damage it could do attacking this vital organ. We wasted no time; Kevin dealt with the tentacle while Lyn and I battered it with energy, then with the help of both guides we pushed it back through to its own world. A world very different to our own. We didn't have to speak to say it had gone, sunshine from a low evening sun began to penetrate into the lounge and fill it with a natural golden light. Richard stood and watched in amazement.

With the house cleansed and returned to normal, we left. As we went up the road to turn around, I saw several other properties I had visited over the years, it all made sense, more now than ever before.

What was the cause? Why were so many houses affected in a small area? Firstly, they are built on a hill. Something that would have been of great importance in ancient times. Hills and mounds were seen as points where the energy could be brought from the earth to the surface. The whole of this area had been heavily mined. When you mine you disturb that which lives below the surface, and when you ruin its habitat, it seeks alternative accommodation. Or maybe the blasting disturbed its world and allows it to interact with ours and this is where the journey begins. The longer it interacts, the stronger it becomes.

Hag on a Hill

Sometimes when something is odd or really frightening, our mind automatically turns away from it, doesn't want to believe it is really true. What we want to believe is that our world is normal and safe. Not the frightening reality that paranormal circumstances can present us with. This was precisely the case with Dave. For all the things his wife Sally and son Aled were experiencing, he would try and find a logical explanation. The toys that turned on without batteries, that didn't happen. Neither did they talk to his son, keeping him awake at night. The shadows dancing across the outside walls, like strange silhouettes, were merely the moonlight. The strange whisperings were the house settling down for the night.

Then one morning he stepped out of the shower and saw the four elongated scratch marks which extended from his neck to his calf, smearing blood over his body, that was when his bubble of rationalisation burst. Finally, he agreed that there may be a problem and agreed that Sally could ask for help. The help was me.

Everything had started eighteen months earlier, when they had removed some problematic trees from the top of the garden. From here the nightmares began.

Aled's toys would spring to life and talk to him as he tried to sleep, talking in strange metallic sounding voices. A monk-like figure would wait on the top of the stairs for him. He too would come out of the shower with scratches on his back. Always the four deep scratches in places he could barely reach. Sally would hear voices around the house, doors opening and closing. She would sense a figure, as if about to pounce behind her, almost feeling their breath on her neck. Then it would simply fade away.

Without doubt this was something demonic. These are the most frightening of all intruders. They have huge psychic powers. They can think, plan and read minds. Their sole purpose being to stimulate the production of any negative emotion they can. This causes the human to produce an energy burst. To them this is food. The more they devour, the stronger becomes their presence in our world. A place they do not belong. Strange as it may sound, Dave began dreaming about beautiful women. Like sirens they called him on, invading his dream space. Sally, on the other hand, was being told in her dreams that Dave was being unfaithful, with beautiful women. This had the precise impact required, it was causing havoc between them. At the same time, Dave was becoming weaker. When we visited, he looked grey. They were not only causing havoc in the marriage, they were energetically bleeding Dave dry, a vamipiring of his life source, his chi. Something he was very keen to deny.

I arrived with Lyn, Bev and two other mediums. The family were in crisis. It was a warm late summer evening, yet the house was dark, cold and foreboding. The atmosphere made it difficult to breathe. You could feel that whatever was here was searching, reading, looking for any weaknesses we may have, looking for a means of penetrating our energetic fields and gaining more trophy victims.

It was difficult to know where to start. This foreboding energy was everywhere in the house, in every room. We stood in the child's bedroom in silence, as we aligned our energies with each other and to the room. As we did so, one of the toys began to move just a little, a robotic toy slowly turned its head to the left, then to the middle, to the right and then back to the middle, it almost seemed to smile. It was indeed as if whatever was here was literally toying with us. Yes, I am here.

It was in the adults' bedroom where I sensed their dreams. They were shocked, and it was as if a light went on for Dave. He looked at me quizzically, asking, 'How did you know that?'

'They have just told me,' I said, pointing upwards.

'That is so true,' he said, shaking his head in amazement. It was going to be easier from this point on. We had Dave on board, this was now going to make our life much easier.

We all continued to walk around the house together, with Sally and Dave.

We decided to begin to try and tackle whatever was here in a small room off the kitchen, and below the bathroom, where all the injuries were occurring. When the moment was right, we sealed off the house, trapping the demon in the room with us. With the help of our Guides, we began to open an etheric gateway back to hell to try to push this thing through. We sensed more than one. With the other side, we had enough power to do this. Then suddenly the room began to grow colder and colder. You could feel the presence of pure evil beginning to build in the room. It was here. Not afraid and ready to do battle. I suddenly heard an urgent voice in my head. 'Do not look at it. Shut your eyes tightly and keep them shut.' I urgently passed this message on to everyone. Checking they understood. They did not open their eyes until I told them to. With the help of the other side, we began to fight to push these entities from our world. We were stabbed with physical pain, made to feel afraid. But we battled on with our eyes firmly shut. And we won.

As we did, the room began to feel brighter and warmer. 'Open your eyes,' I was told, and repeated this to the others. I looked down, and there was the family's young dog. I hadn't noticed that it had come into the room. It sat as if in a trance, fixated on nothing. Whatever it had seen, it had wet itself and was sitting in its own urine, unaware of what it had done. Dave said the dog was very clean and had never had an accident in the house, yet here it was frightened to such an extent it was still sitting in its own water. To Dave this was proof that there had been something, and now it was gone.

Trees are mystical objects. They do so much more than we realise, such as, trap or cap negative energy. Removing the trees had allowed darkness from centuries past to roam freely. Unfortunately, Dave and Sally's house was in the wrong place at the wrong time.

Footnote: This area in question, I found out later, had a history of black magic and witches' covens. The 'ley' in the name ley lines, indicates powerful telluric energetic lines. We believed that whatever was here was associated with the witches. While presenting as beautiful women, we believed they were in fact Hags, and a powerful black monk, faceless Demons with immense power. We believed these were evil ugly Hags. Alongside them was a powerful faceless Monk. (A Monk is often a disguise for very powerful Demons, who shroud themselves in monk like cloaks.

We would over a two-year period return to this property several times. Once, when there was some digging in the street, this seemed to act as a trigger and things returned with a vengeance. We were soon to get this under control again.

On another occasion, more trees were cut down, not by the family but by neighbours. This, again, triggered problems. On this occasion faces could be seen forming in the floor of the bathroom. They would come and go as if the floor was almost made of some substance that enabled it to move and change forms.

In the Beginning

It was very early in my career working as a ghost clearer that I began to understand the significance and importance of children in managing situations.

Paul and I had a couple of friends who had moved to a house in the Telford area. While there were remnants of energy throughout the house indicating that there had indeed been some sort of presence within the property, nothing could be found in any room.

This was quite surprising really considering some of the experiences that the family had been through. This had ranged from kettles melting when they were not plugged into a power source, to barstools spinning on the breakfast bar. There had also been the mystery fire which the fire service had been unable to determine the cause. Their youngest child Molly was becoming increasingly terrified, screaming without just cause and marks would begin to appear on her arms. This had been the final straw; the distress Molly was experiencing had prompted Emily to seek help. Fortunately for Emily I had appeared in a national magazine, and from there she had tracked me down through Facebook.

Yet as hard as we looked, we could find nothing to indicate that there was a problem in the house. All four of us came to the same conclusion. Rather disappointed having travelled so far to deal with the problem, we merely cleared the energies from the house.

The next morning, I had a phone call back from Emily, saying it was back and things were even worse. I was really in a dilemma, as it was clear that there was nothing in the house and yet for what she was describing — slamming doors throughout the house — there appeared to be a problem. I was about to dismiss her problems as not been related to paranormal activity, when a voice in my head prompted me to ask Emily a question. I asked Emily if, as agreed, she had not discussed an impending visit in the house. Emily humbly admitted that she had been discussing this with her husband an hour before we arrived.

I promised to visit the next day, which Paul and I duly did. During the last visit to young children, a little boy, Robert, aged just over two, and Molly, the ten-month-old little girl, had been left with a father who lived just a few doors down. Before ending the conversation, I asked Emily if she and her husband could ensure that the little boy was in the property when we arrived. It wasn't clear why, but experience has taught me to listen to what the spirit world is asking of me.

When we arrived, Craig was sitting shyly on his mom's lap, sucking his dummy. I was in despair, not quite understanding why I needed to speak to this little boy and was convinced that the conversation would prove to be futile. Prompted by my guide White Feather, I casually said to the little boy, 'Do you know any nasty men?'

Well, it was almost as if I had triggered something inside of him and the response was truly astounding. He removed his dummy from his mouth, swivelled round on his mom's lap and then went into great detail to tell me that the nasty man was upstairs in his sister's bedroom and he was hiding from me. Mom and dad were absolutely astounded by this conversation. I found out so much information from that little boy just by asking simple questions. One of the questions I asked was whether he frightened his sister. During the last visit Emily had told us that Molly would scream as if in agony, real tears running down her cheeks and red marks would appear on her arms. It was thought at first that Craig was scratching his sister, though the majority of the time he was nowhere to be seen when these events occurred. Craig's little face lit up, and forming claw-like hands and grimacing his face, he ran across the room, demonstrating how the nasty man frightened his sister and then proceeded to pinch as if he was scratching little arms. 'Is this what he does?' I asked. He nodded. Feeling quite pleased with how much information this little boy was able to give me, I asked him if he knew what had happened on my previous visit. Immediately he told me that, yes, nasty man had known I was coming and had hidden in the house over the road with the other ghosts. Father Ben was astounded. Long before he and

Emily had got together, there had been a piece in a local paper concerning an alleged haunting that had taken place at the house his little boy was pointing at. The conversation between Craig and myself lasted about fifteen minutes, and throughout this time mom and dad were totally astounded by his ability to be able to communicate with me. Startled looks went between the two of them and on several occasions they both advised me that he couldn't speak, he was behind with his talking. Well, I have to say not on this occasion. He was determined to tell me, and I was more than willing to listen. He used his arms to gesture size, pointed to areas in the house and grimaced his face to imitate that of the 'nasty man'. By the time he had finished talking he was quite pleased with himself. All the time mom and dad listened with faces that moved from utter amazement to laughter and joy, as they shifted their gazes from the little boy to each other.

We said our goodbyes to Craig, and off he went to grandad's. Then, as advised by Craig, we found the 'nasty man' hiding in his sister's bedroom. He had nowhere to go, busted by a child who apparently couldn't talk.

On this occasion I refused to engage and listen to his tale of woe or to offer sympathy or empathy. I felt he was a bully and had tormented this family long enough. It was time for him to go.

I did hear from Emily around about four weeks later. She rang to tell me life had returned to normal, and the house was settled. From this point on, Craig never mentioned the nasty man again.

This was an important lesson for me. I had always made a point of asking for the children under the age of eighteen to be out of the property when we visited, not wishing to expose them to any further turmoil or the risk of contamination from psychic interaction.

From here on I understood that it was not for me to decide what was best for the children. I should listen to what the guides had to say to me, and when prompted, to seek the views of the little ones in the house.

I was never disappointed, except for the one occasion when the little girl was too terrified to speak out in fear of retribution from the darkness residing in her home. On every other occasion they never failed to help me, guide me, and with no airs and graces, directly tell me if I had failed to fully remove the Ghost from the property.

'No, it is still here' is quite demoralising to hear when you have worked for half the evening to move something on, and you're convinced you had achieved what you set out to do.

'Are you sure?' I have asked on more than one occasion, only to hear the child emphatically tell me yes and point to where the ghost is standing, sometimes right in front of us.

Mommy, Make Him Go Away

Looking back, I'm still unsure how Pippa got my number. I received a phone call just after Christmas. Pippa lived with Carl in a three-bedroomed Council house on the Dudley/Sandwell Border. For quite a while they had been having problems in the house. But over the last few weeks it had got exceedingly worse. Pippa found herself not sleeping, and her children's sleep disturbed on a regular basis. There is no doubt that children being born at the moment appear to be more psychically aware. A 'sensitive' child can be disturbed for a variety of reasons, including dreams, energies and atmospheres around them. I spoke to Pippa for quite a while on the phone and during this discussion it became apparent that there may be more going on here than a sensitive child being disturbed by earthly matters. Most definitely these appeared to be unearthly issues here!

Our team of four set off on the only free night we had between us. In the cold and rain, we gathered together outside the house. As usual I had only told them as much as they needed to know. It was the same for myself, I only asked what I needed to know and usually stopped the person from telling me too much so I couldn't be influenced by their version of events.

We entered the property together and began trying to relax the nervous couple. Would you to like to sit down or have a drink? was always met with a definite no. We always began to work the moment we arrived in the property. Sitting down and relaxing was not the way to do it. Now sometimes, while whatever is in the property has been fearless, this is often not the case when we arrive. They will often try and hide from you, re-appearing after we have left. Now being wise to this trick, we immediately sealed the property from the inside. This involves visualising silver light covering the inside walls, ceilings and floors. This ensures that whatever is in the property is firmly held within the walls. This way we can be sure of dealing with it in one go, negating the need to come back again.

We passed a brief period of time with small talk. Within minutes we were all of the same mind — the problem lay upstairs, not downstairs. Pippa confirmed this. We then began to walk around the rooms. The rear child's bedroom definitely appeared to be where we needed to be, although the bathroom, hallway and just inside the front bedroom also appeared to be quite negative. In full agreement, we all stood in the back bedroom and slowly began to try and bring together exactly what had been happening here. We knew from Pippa that her youngest daughter couldn't sleep and was complaining of a man being in her bedroom. This was the only information we had been given at our request. We need not have worried about sealing the property, as this man had no intentions of hiding from us. He boldly made himself known to us. He was angry, arrogant and aggressive. His whole persona was hostile. It soon became apparent what effect he was having on the whole family.

Quite interestingly the husband never felt his presence. This entity had targeted his wife and children, the most vulnerable ones, keeping well hidden from the husband. Sometimes the easiest way to deal with an entity is to bring them out, to get them communicating with us. This is done for several reasons. In most cases they do not mean any harm. Sometimes it is a ham-fisted way to try and communicate with the living. The entity has died. They may not know they have died, or they do not understand what is happening to them. Any attempts to rescue them from the spirit world fail, as the entity is afraid or doesn't understand what is happening, so they will try and communicate with those around them. This often results in the occupants of the property being scared witless and they do not know what is happening to them. It is the element of the unknown; they don't know the abilities of this entity or its capabilities. This is what makes the situation quite frightening.

We began to try and communicate with this man. He immediately began to make himself known to us. As Mediums it is quite easy to begin to communicate, or at the very least begin to pick up elements of the entity's character. Here we had a man whose life had been cut short; he was a man who was very strict with his family, his daughters and his wife. A man who was fond of the sauce, in this case the sauce was alcohol. He was someone who had departed this plane before he felt ready to do so. At the point of death, when the gateway opened, he had refused to go, deciding to stay here instead, wandering around in search of the taste for alcohol. There were obviously connections with the house or a neighbouring property. What was also clear was he was too terrified to depart this plane and face his maker.

What was apparent was the anger which appeared to drip off him. Have you or the girls been arguing much? I asked. The answer was affirmative. Apparently as soon as all the girls gathered in this room, they began to fight, nowhere else. At other times all three of them got on well, but never here in this room. Pippa also admitted that things were extremely tense between her and her husband. She explained he made her feel very angry, especially when they were in the bedroom. Completely out of character she had found herself hitting out at her husband. We were not surprised.

Together we opened a doorway into the next world and asked him to go forward. He was adamant that he would not go through the doorway, and we were adamant he would. But he was trapped. Once inside the room we had sealed the room with silver light. He could not escape from us. He searched the party, looking for weaknesses. His first victim was Karen. Within seconds she began to feel panic rise up in her.

'I'm sorry, but I am really afraid,' she said. You could hear the fear in her voice. 'I am not sure I can carry on. This thing is pressing down on my back, and I am struggling to breath.'.

Karen had done this for many years, she was a seasoned Cleanser. He had found the weakest link. You could feel his rancid breath breathing down on her and he moved as close as he could. Sensing his victory, he moved closer. Suddenly from nowhere Karen seemed to grow in size. 'I am not going to be terrorised by this,' she almost spat, and in a second, she knocked him away from her. Before he had chance to turn on anyone else, we grabbed him. We circled him in light, spun him round so he could not move and almost physically threw him through a grey portal. The 'other side' were waiting to receive. They would deal with him from now on.

We needed no confirmation. The terrified Pippa, who had witnessed the whole thing from the protected space of the landing, gave out a sigh. 'That feels better,' she said, before we had time to confirm between us all that he had actually gone through the doorway.

We walked from room to room checking that he was nowhere to be seen or felt. We then began to replace the dense negative energy in the bedrooms with much lighter energy. We showered each room with gold and silver confetti.

As we checked Pippa and her husband's room, Pippa told us a story. A woman lived close by who was a psychic herself. Pippa had a dream the woman was pregnant. So she had told the woman this. Unfortunately, at four months pregnant she lost the baby. Pippa had felt extremely guilty about this. Blaming herself and wondering if she hadn't told her, would the woman have ever known she was pregnant? Or would she have lost the baby without realising it, thus never going through the great sense of loss as you cannot mourn what you don't know you have?

What was more startling, was that the entity appeared to somehow know of this guilt. Pippa saw it on more than one occasion, standing in the window, pointing at this woman's house, shaking his finger. This action added to her feeling of guilt and was a reminder to the shame Pippa felt.

Why would a spirit do this to her? Was it the that the production of negative energy gave it something to feed off? I believe it does. For negative entities the production of a negative emotion created fuel for their own growth. This is what was happening here, the more afraid or guilty the family felt, the more energy they produced.

This does not make this entity evil, just someone who is continuing in the pattern of life they had before. Ruling the females around him by instigating fear in them and living off their pain. Whereas previously gloating in his dominance, here he was feeding his physic power in order to grow.

We left the property forty-five minutes later, leaving behind a much calmer and peaceful wife and bedrooms with an energy and vibration conducive for sleeping peacefully in. Certainly more peaceful, than when we arrived. To all intents and purposes, it remained that way the last time we heard.

Respecting the Land

Louise was very frightened when she called me at first. She spoke very quickly, making it difficult to understand. Things were so bad in her house, her partner and child had fled the previous evening and refused to return. At first, I was finding it hard to find out what the problem was, but the more she spoke, the more I understood. Louise found it hard to come to terms with the reality that there was a problem with her lovely home. A lot of activity centred around her four-year-old son Harvey. A friend who was also a Medium had been to the house and appeared to have been quite successful, as for a while it calmed down. He believed Harvey was possessed. This did not sit comfortably with me, but I agreed to visit.

On the days leading up to the visit I became more alarmed as Louise, through text, began to show me the full extent of the problem. This very gifted four-year-old could see it all. Despite being told not to talk to Mommy, he began to confide in her. He described the ruler as being the Queen. The others had to obey whatever she said. Next there was a man with half his face burnt off and a man made up of shadows. He told her there were lots more. I soon began to realise there were an awful lot more than I had first realised. I also knew this little boy was being 'allowed' to talk to his mommy, so I understood the extent of the problem.

This was further shown to me the previous night, during a meditation. Right at the beginning I was given the word 'Demi-god', followed by a Demi-god. I didn't need telling twice. On the day of the visit, I looked up the term and found loads of them. I was drawn to Zeus and Hercules. I tuned in to them and requested their help should we need them. Later that night I was glad I had.

We were all surprised to find this mid-terrace house set in a small village in Shropshire, nestling in the middle of a small estate of modern houses. Designed to match the setting of the village, these houses were tastefully designed to fit into the 'olde-worlde' image of this area, whose roots could be traced back to the Doomsday book.

As we stood sealing the property, this tastefully presented property began to change, a foreboding feeling passed over me and a stillness, as if the house was waiting for our presence — inviting us in, but for all the wrong reasons. I felt a shiver pass over me. I increased the strength of my cloak of protection and beckoned the others to do the same.

As agreed, Louise was in the house with her partner Charlie, Harvey (her son) and a friend's daughter was also there. I had asked Louise if I could talk to Harvey, but I didn't want him present during the clearance, so Charlie was going to take him round her mother's house, which was nearby. The house was in fact in the same row and unbeknown to us was facing similar problems.

After saying all our greetings to each other, I began to quiz Harvey. He wouldn't speak to me or look at me, or any of the others. I knew 'the Queen' was close by and he was more afraid of her than any mortal, including his mother. He point-blank refused to speak to me. After much cajoling we began a communication system. I would ask the question. He would whisper the answer into his mother's ear. 'Are the Queen and her people here, Harvey?' I asked. Yes, he confirmed, conveyed through the whisper. 'Where are they?' In his room, Louise relayed. Kevin, Lyn and Patrick nodded and smiled. This had confirmed what we already suspected. 'Where are the others?' I asked.

'Above the light bulb,' came the reply through Louise. Which confirmed what we suspected: more were hiding in the attic. You could see Harvey was terrified but continued to duly tell his mom. The previous night he had told Louise if she let anyone else come into the house, she would bring more and hurt them badly and she could kill them if she wished.

We bade Harvey and Charlie goodbye and promised when they returned, the house would be back to normal.

Feeling we had wasted enough time and with the others chaffing at the bit, raring to go, we made our way upstairs. With each step you took you could feel the atmosphere changing. As we walked, swirls of cold energy seemed to whip around are faces. The atmosphere felt charged, as fear engulfed if you let it. We made our way to Harvey's room. We placed Louise and Dave in between us. I could feel Dave's uncertainty. I placed him with Paul. His cool, level- headed approach would ensure he never took his eye off Dave, protecting him to the end. This was Paul's strength, and I intended to use it so that nothing stopped us from dealing with this darkness.

We stood in the bedroom, without the main light on. I turned off the fish tank light and pump to reduce distraction and began to tune in. As I stood, I could see a line of energy zigzagging across the room. It entered the house, in the middle of the couple's bedroom, bounced into the bathroom, then passed diagonally across Harvey's bedroom. This line reached high into the attic and was constantly active, with a steady supply of energy passing through. But then rather oddly it was flowing back, passing more energy, mingling together and creating vortices in several places in the house and surrounding land. Some of it was flowing, but a lot was trapped. I began to ask my Guide White Feather what was happening. I was shown in my mind's eye a very old-fashioned dam, as if a stream had been blocked. I could clearly see the silver blocks held into place by the blackness. Somehow someone had blocked the flow of this energy through the ley lines, creating a dam of energy which had in the past been used for performing black magic. The people with these skills had long gone, but the vortices lived on, causing no harm to anyone, until these houses were built upon the land. The occupants were now sitting right on top of darkness conjured up aeons ago, and it was here to stay. I could now see their power source. We would deal with that later.

We began to tune in. I instructed the others to look for the Queen, I knew she wouldn't hide from us, she was afraid of no one. Lyn was the first to speak.

'Sandrea, I can see a black figure, she almost looks like a witch,' she said.

Kevin added, 'She is huge and very powerful.' The others nodded in agreement.

'Oh my God,' Louise said, 'that's what Harvey says, he sees a witch too.' She was a shape shifter. For the moment she decided to show herself in all her glory as a hideous Hag. I could feel her sitting right in the middle of the bed. Her energy shifted from over seven feet in height down to about five feet. I asked the others where she was, simultaneously they all pointed to the bed, where I sensed her. I tuned my energies into her, and as I did, I felt her rise up and send a bolt of energy at me. It hit me directly in the chest. I lost my footing for a moment and fell backwards. My head was killing me. Here she had shown her power and what she was capable of. After a few moments I was okay, the group were all concerned about what she had done to me. I reassured them I was okay and instructed the others to pull their guides closer. I gave them the choice of either Zeus or Hercules to help them. I brought in the Rock, a mass of black energy made to fight darkness. I was given him to use whenever I felt the need but was advised to use him sparingly. Well, tonight was going to be one of those nights. Noises could be heard all over the house, it was if it was creaking and moving on its foundations as the light and the dark battled each other. In unison we reigned fireball after fireball onto her. We were no match for her, but these Demi-gods were. After about five minutes she was too weak to fight any more, and unable to flee as we held her in the room. I saw a tube of light descend into the room. We were to push her into it to avoid her finding a way of staying. The other side stood waiting to greet her. It took a further five minutes to finally push her down the tube. Immediately it disappeared. We then began to search the room for the others. I could see something darting across the floor. I asked the others, 'Did you see that?'

'Looked like a rat,' Patrick said. Then there was another, then another.

'I thought it was a spider,' Kevin added.

Lyn smiled and said, 'Both.'

Again, Louise chimed in. 'That's what Harvey says he sees, spiders and rats scurrying across his bedroom and ours.' We swept the upper floor, catching lots of these and throwing them through another doorway.

Next, we pulled down from the attic. Here we had three small entities, a cross between a gargoyle and an elf, including the one that had half a face. Together we worked in catching these things and throwing them over. We found another one hiding in the parents' bedroom and two more downstairs in the living room. As we finished each room, you could feel the temperature rise immediately and the rooms became brighter. This was nothing to us, but Louise and Dave were amazed by the transformation in their home. We knew we had to do something to stop this from coming back in again. So we removed the dam and built shields all around the house.

Two hours later we had finished. We had one more test to pass. What would Harvey think? Louise called Charlie and asked her to bring Harvey round. We took him upstairs into his bedroom, the place that had been the centre of activity. He looked around and then said, 'There is a spider.' My heart fell, until I noticed he was pointing to an actual spider, nestled up the corner. Dad smiled at me, and I smiled back.

The next day Louise contacted me. She thought there was something in Emma's house, Charlie's mom. At first, I was not convinced, although she sent me enough to get me to change my mind. 'Can you come and look at ours again? Harvey is saying the spiders are back.'

Cautiously I asked, 'You haven't been round to Emma's, have you?'

'Yes, I took the photographs.' I groaned and explained that by doing so, she had invited it back in. At the moment it was only the energy, but in time it would be other things too.

So, two weeks later we returned to this sleepy village, which we later learnt held very strong connections to the persecution of witches. Firstly, we went to Emma's house, then back to Louise's.

A lot of the activity seemed to be focused around Charlie and her bedroom, which was situated at the front of the house, directly in alignment to Harvey's bedroom.

Almost as soon as we began to work, the dog started to become very agitated; he was running around the house, then he began to claw frantically at the door to a cupboard on the landing, almost ripping up the carpet. We exchanged glances at each other have learnt over the years to follow what animals were trying to show us. There is was another Gargoyle like creature hiding in the cupboard, hoping to miss detection. The dog had other ideas. We were soon able to dispel this horrid creature back to the world it belonged. There was clearly a sprit path between the properties and these entities had been using this to transverse from one property to another.

Charlie's had attachments in her stomach, currently under medical investigation for problems in this area. This problem had only developed while she lived in this house. Miraculously as the dark entities were removed, so were Charlie's health problems. They simply disappeared.

Retribution from the Past

Kendy, his wife Anita and their two children lived two hundred yards from his parents, with his sister living an equal distance in the other direction. The significance of this would not become apparent until after we had visited Kendy's house.

He lived in a fairly modern mid-terrace house, where older properties had once stood. It would seem they had lived with a list of problems for over two years. Things had come to a head when their two-day old baby returned from hospital and screamed constantly when she was taken into the big back bedroom, only quietening down when taken out of the room. After two nights, in desperation, the whole family moved into the front bedroom. This suited Kendy, as twice when sleeping in the back bedroom he had woken to find himself pinned to the bed and unable to move for several minutes. This had also happened to him in broad daylight. Several times the eldest boy talked of seeing a man on the landing and in his room, and asked his puzzled mother why this nasty man kept coming into their house and frightening him. Kendy had not been able to work for a while now, due to the sensation of thousands of ants running over the back of his head, affecting his ability to concentrate. As a taxi driver, his powers of concentration were imperative.

Kendy had found a single apple in the middle of his lawn, full of blood, with no explanation of how this could have got there into his secluded garden. On another occasion, late one evening he found his white car covered in spots of blood.

We decided to start by visiting the area of the garden where the apple was found. To the rear of this were lots of tall trees, hiding the part which lay behind. Almost as if they were trying to help us, the tops of the trees swayed in circular motions. Yet on that cool September evening there was no breeze. Lyn's words echoed my views. 'Remember the property in Sedgley?' she asked. I nodded. We now knew the source of where it was coming from, it was travelling through the trees. Satisfied we were beginning to understand some of the issues, we went into the lounge. As with many properties like this, the room was dark and dank, cold with different horrible smells passing through, including stale tobacco, yet neither party smoked.

'The man next door does,' Kendy added. As stupid as this sounds, I then knew I needed to stretch our search beyond this house. How could that be? Flowing through and covering the houses either side, we were on a portal, a crossover of two energy lines, and it seemed this was quite a large opening to cover three properties.

We decided to follow our instinct and to begin by exploring the upper floor. As we walked up the stairs, the lighting was so poor we could barely see the stairs. I stopped and looked up at the single bright bulb. It was throwing lots of light out, yet the light couldn't penetrate the atmosphere. So cautiously we climbed the stairs. We were all drawn to the rear purple bedroom, only to discover this was the room where Kendy had been attacked and the baby cried.

Kevin, Lyn, Patrick and I stood in a semi-circle, with Kendy and Anita carefully placed in between us. As we stood, we began to feel and sense the atmosphere in the room. 'I can see hangings, lots of them,' Kevin said. I knew this belonged to the rear of the property. As I tuned in, I told the group what I could see. I could see a pool of blackness to the rear of the property, as if all the evil deeds of the past were contained, held together, festering. This blackness was seeping into the property. I also felt as if there were mines underneath the property allowing this blackness to seep and move. Kendy confirmed that the whole area was built on mines. In fact, there was a mine shaft in the park directly beyond their house. Tunnels deep in the ground act like ley lines and allow the energy to flow in places where they wouldn't normally. I felt this darkness had started as a result of someone practising black magic. The people had long gone and no traces of their existence could be found in the physical world or the history books, but their cauldron of darkness remained tormenting any occupants who happened to be within reach of it.

We began to try and isolate and contain this source, focusing on the middle of the bed. As we did, we could feel it begin to grow. In sharp steps the room began to grow darker and darker and the feeling came over us all that we couldn't breathe properly as this huge energy began to make its presence known to us. Now it was moving from the unseen world into the seen. A black mass could be seen forming on the bed, growing bigger and more powerful. As I looked at it, I could see snakes slithering across the bed. Circling around us. No matter how far they moved, they all stayed connected to the central pool of darkness. Not wishing to alarm Kendy or Anita, I casually mentioned the snakes. Lyn looked across at me, with her knowing look that told me she could see what I could see, the others nodded too.

'Oh my God, my son talks of snakes all the time. He says he can see them all over floor and in my daughter's cot.'

Kendy added, 'Mom had those too.' I didn't ask any more. I could feel its power and I knew we were in trouble. There were four of us. This was much more powerful that we could deal with. I told Kendy and Anita to ignore me, just for a moment. They nodded in agreement. I then turned to the others and with an urgency in my voice said we didn't have enough power to fight this beast. Without emotion, Lyn agreed. Our most powerful member could also feel this was greater than us. Quickly I instructed them all to pull their guides in as close as they could. I called in the Rock. I rarely used him, but tonight I needed him. I felt his black mass begin to form to my right. I told Kevin, to bring in 'The Fire' and instructed Patrick and Lyn to work with Zeus and Hercules (see Footnote).

We began to attack this beast, but as we began to destroy the snakes, more and more appeared. Lyn said, 'It's Hydra, as we destroy it, so more will grow.'

Kevin quickly added, "Use the fire." So we did. And we slowly began to break down this beast. The more we reined on it, the smaller it became, it slowly began to diminish, until it was too weak to fight any more.[1]

The other side understood more than we did exactly what we had here. I saw a long, thin tunnel begin to appear in the room. Not of the bright light we were used to, this was of the darkness. It was as if they were sending a transport system from here in this room back to their own world and they were not taking any chances of this escaping and staying here in our world. The tunnel hovered above this darkness. All we had to do was push it towards this opening and they would do the rest. So we did, with one last final push, using physical energy and mind control we manoeuvred this beast towards the tunnel. A further battle pursued, until

---

[1] I later discovered Hercules slayed Hydra by using fire to stop the heads from growing back. Also, that Hydra was known for its poisonous blood.

eventually we had it in the tube. Within minutes powerful guardians from the other side pulled it through, taking it from our world and moving it into its own world. 'I feel a bit funny, lightheaded, as if something is pulling me,' Kendy said.

It confirmed what I already knew, this thing was embedded into Kendy's energy field and was hanging on for dear life. I turned to Kendy and said, 'I know it's hard, but just be brave for a few moments longer, then it will be gone forever.'

I could see he trusted me, he believed me. This helped him to withstand this discomfort for a few moments longer. After what seemed like a long battle, it was gone. Before we could confirm this Anita said, 'Oh my goodness, it is so much lighter in here.' And it was. We swept the room and exchanged the energy. Then we sealed it. We moved to the next bedroom. This was the smallest of them all and belonged to the little boy. It was dark, cold and horrid.

'Does he sleep in here?' I asked.

'Never,' they both chimed together. Anita went on to explain in their former home he had, but since they had arrived here, he had refused to sleep in the room, or even play in there, complaining a man watched over him. I knew the man they were talking about, he still stood here in the room. He looked like the character Fagin, with his ugly face, hooked nose and protruding rotting teeth. He clothes belonged to the seventeenth century. He was nowhere near as powered as the

143

previous beast, but he wielded power. The power to evoke fear. He was not the darkness but a long time ago he had become trapped by it, now he was part of it. As we stood in the room, tuning in and trying to decide how to deal with him, he suddenly reared up, making himself three times bigger than his normal size and became even more menacing as he grew in size. He lunged at me, stopping a few inches from my face. He grimaced his face and growled at me. His power caught me off guard and threw me against the wall. As I moved back, his sinister face followed me. After seconds I regained my feet. While he was big, he was vulnerable. They became even more menacing, others needed no command. They could either see or sense him. They had seen what he had done to me. As I pulled in the power, so did they and collectively we overpowered him. We used the Demi-Gods from the previous room and with the help of the Fire Guardian and the Rock, we knocked it from our world and sent him tumbling back into his own, through a hastily produced dark tube. As we sent him, we swept the room, throwing through remnants of his dark energy with him. Instantaneously the room began to grow brighter and warmer.

We quickly moved on, into the next bedroom. We were tiring and needed to finish before our energy ran out. This was the parents' bedroom, where they had moved into, with their children. The energy was nowhere near as bad as the other rooms. As we scanned, we saw small black spiders scurrying across the room, running up and down the walls, trying to hide in the corners of the room. We checked and scanned to ensure there was nothing else in the room. There wasn't, it was clear. We checked with each other, we were all agreed nothing else was here. I asked them all to describe what they could see. Patrick spoke first. 'They are horrible, like black spiders, with fur.'

Lyn nodded. Kevin added, 'They are everywhere.' Anita explained that is what her son described. Kendy added one had run over him last week, as he lay awake in bed. We decided to trawl the room together and catch them in one go. Well, so we thought, in fact it took several attempts before we managed to catch them all. Satisfied we were done, we moved onto the landing, which was now bright, and we could see the stairs, not like before, when they seemed so dark.

We moved downstairs and began to check the bottom floor. There did not appear to be anything living here. But the energy poured in from behind the houses, with a line running in the opposite direction, creating a powerful vortex. This swirling pool of energy was contaminated from a black pool of energy. We stood tuning in. 'I feel hangings, lots of them,' Kevin said. The others agreed. I could sense darkness, I could see tunnels under the ground.

'Was there any mining around here?' Kendy explained there was a mine shaft in the park at the bottom of the garden. I could sense bad deeds, but not of recent, this was dating back many, many years.

Possibly before records were kept. Somehow this had been gathered into a pool of stagnant dark energy, it was horrible. And it was seeping into this vortex, contaminating it.

I moved my energy towards this pool. Gently but firmly, I was warned to stay away. It was too much for us to handle, the other side would deal with this, now we had removed some of the occupants from the putrid pool. Our job here was to cleanse this vortex and block the pool from entering into it. If we failed, the doorway through to hell would remain permanently open. So we began by cutting off the access into this vortex. We sealed and contained the pool. We then began to purify the vortex, washing it with clean energy, dissolving the blackness. As we did, so the room became lighter and cleaner. At last, we had finished. The house had returned to normal.

We finished by cleansing both Anita and Kendy, removing the mass from the back of his head, purifying him and cleansing this aura. Anita was lucky there did not appear to be anything in her energy field, it seemed their victim had been Kendy.

After two and a half hours our work was finally done. As we got ready to leave, I asked Kendy why he had bought this house. I knew his mom and dad lived down the road, but why this one? 'It was cheap, I mean really cheap,' he said. It had been empty, for ages.

I looked at him and smiled and said, 'That figures.'

Smiling, he said, 'I know.'

Three days later Kendy was back on the phone. 'I think it is back,' he said. He went on to tell me the house had been great, but he had gone to visit his mom and the sensation to his head returned and now the house didn't feel right again. As strange as it sounded it would seem his mom and dad, who lived two hundred yards away, had also been having terrible problems. Kendy forgot to mention this. Now it had found a way back in, through his parents. So another date was set to go to his parents' house and start all over again. Afterwards we would go back to Kendy's and seal it down again.

He did go on to say the day after our visit his next-door neighbour had told him, he felt great for the first time in years his kids had slept through the night and were really happy, not fighting or anything.

Ruined Garden

Emma's situation came to me via an Avon collection. Dean, my close friend and fellow ghost hunter, had been to collect an Avon order, when Emma's sister showed him a very strange picture. From the kitchen Emma had taken a picture of Joshua, her youngest son, riding around the garden on his little bike. Several days later Emma was browsing through the pictures on her phone and was really shocked to see another child alongside her son. When she had taken the picture Joshua was alone in the garden. On closer inspection, Emma and her husband Chris saw something was not right. The second mystery child was almost a replica of their son and at first the family thought the camera had somehow created an image of their little boy. Despite appearing to be identical, there were some distinct differences between the two little boys. Joshua had gloves on, the second child did not. Neither was he on the bike. More strangely the second child appeared to be walking with both his knees bent and his feet did not appear to be in contact with the ground. Around the fence in the background several faces, quite ghoulish in appearance, could be quite clearly made out.

After viewing the picture, I agreed to go and visit the family to try and discover what was happening. The family had also reported the little boy was seeing invisible people in the house. I had enough to convince me a visit was required and also, I was curious to understand what was happening here.

Paul, Patrick, Dean, Lyn and myself all arrived together. We were greeted warmly by the family. Several of the group had not seen the photograph, so Chris loaded it onto his phone and shared it with us. We chatted to the family about some of the other incidents. It would seem Joshua could see and was talking to Chris's mother, who had passed long before he was born. He had told Chris all about his mom and despite his scepticism Chris was convinced Joshua was somehow communicating with his mother. As we were about to leave the room, Patrick asked for a copy of the picture. Chris reloaded it and was shocked to see the mystery child had disappeared from the photograph. We could all see it for our own eyes. There was not a trace of the child in the picture.

We walked around the lower rooms and we were all in agreement there did not appear to be anything untoward. There were no cold spots, smells, etc. In fact, it felt very normal. That is until you looked into the back garden; something did not feel right. I asked Emma to point out precisely where Joshua was when the picture was taken. It was roughly in the area where both Lyn and I had felt drawn to. We decided to go out to the garden. Emma began to apologise for the state of the garden. Over the last two years she had spent several thousands of pounds. But nothing survived. They had purchased a top-grade lawn, yet it was bald in places, and in the very centre, where Joshua had been standing, the grass was sparse and patchy with several areas where there was no grass. Emma went on the say she had replaced it twice and the same always happened. No matter how they fed the lawn, they could not get grass to grow in the middle. The garden was lined with hanging baskets, yet very little sprouted from them. The borders were barren of any greenery or flowers. It seemed Emma was a keen gardener, but nothing would grow in this garden, now she had resigned herself to it, she had given up.

We walked around the garden. You could feel a strange stillness around the centre of the garden. A gentle breeze was blowing, but not in the centre of the garden. The trees and shrubs around us swayed in the gentle breeze, but nothing was felt around the centre. I looked at the washing line running down the middle of the garden. I then turned to Emma and asked her a rather strange question. 'Emma,' I said, 'How does your washing dry?' My question clearly threw her for a second.

She then turned to me and said, 'Well, funny you have asked, it doesn't. I have given up putting it out now. It can be out all day and yet it doesn't dry.' She then added. 'My family think I'm mad when I tell them.'

I wasn't surprised and neither were the others, the problem was definitely relating to the ground.

In most cases the problem is an energy line, an opening or a portal. In such cases the area is normally energised and can clearly be felt. In this case there was nothing but a rather strange stillness.

We decided to try and tune in and see what we could discover. We left the rest of the family inside and kept Emma with us in the garden. Lyn was the first to speak, she said she could feel water underground and a cavern. She turned to Emma and asked her if she had any knowledge of water in the vicinity. She confirmed there was water running under the house. They had discovered this when they extended the dining area.

We were all in agreement, this was not evil or dark, but something was wrong. Between us we began to use our physic gifts to probe deep into the ground under the garden. All five of us joined in, exchanging information with each other.

We found a cavern directly underneath the garden. There we could see a pool of black stagnant rancid water. As if to confirm, we began to smell the most atrocious pungent smell of stale dirty water, it was horrible. Patrick was the first to notice it, then Emma, who stood to his side. 'Oh my God,' she said. 'We get this a lot, we have been to the authorities about it, but no one seems to know where it is coming from. It drives us mad,' she said. It slowly wafted across the whole of the garden until we could all smell it. It was disgusting and we found it difficult to concentrate as we were overcome by it.

Trying to ignore it, we closed our eyes and tuned in again to this underground cavern. I could clearly see the cavern and the water. To the side of this fetid demon, I could see several elementals just sitting there, as if they were at a loss what to do with this pool. I could see several fairies and such like creatures. This seemed to be pushing my belief system to the edge of reason. Before I could speak Lyn and Dean spoke about seeing small fairy-like people around the edge of this pool. Patrick and Paul spoke in agreement. This was not a figment of my imagination; each and every one of us could see and sense the same. If Emma was shocked, she didn't show it. It would seem somehow this pool of water had become contaminated, not by dirt or rubbish. This was infestation from an etheric source. This pool of water had been filled with dark vibration. We felt it had travelled down an energy line and somehow it had become trapped in this pool in this cavern. Such was the contamination, the elementals were unable to cleanse it. They needed the assistance of humans to clear their sacred space. This was not a recent occurrence but something which had built up over a significant period of time. I could sense an infestation from a slaughterhouse. I could feel the fear and pain of hundreds of animals held in this small area, which measured no more than three feet either way. I suspected the contamination stretched deep down into the bowels of the Earth.

Having found the source, we began the process of cleansing. We bombarded the area with light. We used an array of different methods to penetrate deep into the Earth, including crystals wands to boost the power. We sent down shards, arrows, curves, spirals and waves. We continually blasted the area, stopping every few minutes to see if our job was done. After about ten minutes we finally won the battle and you could physically feel the difference. A gentle breeze began to drift over us. We had emptied this fetid pool of negative energy. Despite their mistrust of the human race, the little people, sent their thanks to us. Immediately they began busying themselves, finishing off what we had started. The difference was immediate, even Emma could feel the breeze and it felt quite nice in their garden. The grass under our feet began to change and instantly we could see patches of green grass, which were not there before. We could have kicked ourselves for not taking a picture before we started.

We went back into the house to say our goodbyes and to tell Chris our work was done. Before we left Chris told us he had been watching from the window. He turned to Lyn and I and said, 'You two are the main ones, aren't you?' Before I could answer he talked of seeing a white mist, which was quite distinctive but without a true form. This had been moving around Lyn and I as we were working. I suspected the elementals were projecting images up to us so we could see what was wrong with the ground.

We said our goodbyes and Emma promised to keep us posted with what was happening with the ground. We received several texts, thanking us for our assistance. They reported over the next week more and more grass had grown and the lawn was slowly turning back into the luscious grass it had been when the lawn was first laid down.

As we sat in the pub contemplating the events of the evening, I was still not quite sure about the picture and the fact the little boy disappeared while we were standing there. We then reflected on the experience, the little boy had been discovered on the photograph a few days before Dean's visit. Everyone in the extended family were amazed and they were sharing it with everyone. We came to the conclusion that had been done deliberately. The elementals knew Dean was experienced enough to be able to sense if there was a problem. How clever, we all concluded.

Stuck in the Middle

Over the years I have been contacted in many ways. But I have to say I was a little surprised to receive an e-mail through Facebook asking for assistance. It was the case of a friend of a friend, who knew me and obviously knew more about me than I did about them. Somehow, they had heard about my work ghost busting so they sent a plea for assistance for his step daughter, by Facebook.

Janine and Stuart lived together in a modern Council house, on a modern estate. They had only moved in a couple of months ago, yet already they were beginning to regret this move. Between them they have four children ranging from the age of ten down to a little girl a few months old. It was the seven and three-year-old that seemed to be the victims and targets for the attention of this entity. As soon as I had Janine's telephone number, I called her and asked her to explain to me what was happening. She told me how her seven-year-old son and three-year-old were being tormented by something they couldn't see. At first, she thought it was their imagination, the settling into a new house and the children being children. It got to the point where neither of the middle two children were going upstairs alone or to the toilet, and they were waking up crying throughout the night. It seemed that we really did have a problem on our hands and so I gathered together, Lyn, Kevin, Paul and myself and on a cold Saturday night we set off to try and find out what was going on here. I had asked Janine to keep the children at the house when I visited. This is normally a no-no as I would much rather work without small children in the house, but on this occasion, I felt I needed to talk to the children to find out precisely what was going on to check there were no attachments on them.

As soon as we arrived, we went and sat in the kitchen with mom and the three-year-old Bradley. Janine had said on reflection it was Bradley who was being targeted the most, and in view of this we thought this would be the best starting point. So we all sat there and I tried to coax Bradley into telling me what had been going on. He was very reluctant to talk to me and constantly asked his mom to tell me what was happening, but even Janine knew it was important that I heard it from his mouth so understood what was happening. Eventually after much cajoling he began to talk to me. In his childlike language he said there were three people in the house, besides the family. One was a young girl, and by all accounts she seemed to be about the age of twelve years old. She had on one occasion pushed him down the stairs. He told us how he lay at the bottom of the stairs crying and she stood on the stairs laughing at him. She also kept calling him a bitch. He then shyly said, 'She keeps doing this to me,' and he held up two fingers. It didn't take much to work out this was not the solid victory but the flicking of the Vs, so to speak. He went on to tell us how they kept waking up during the night and he could hear them laughing, and that they were standing outside the toilet waiting for him. I had heard all I needed to hear and did not want to distress Bradley unnecessarily. All four of us reassured him that we were going to get rid of the bad man and the two children, and that by the time I said goodbye to him there would be nothing left in the house.

We placed Stuart and the four children in the lounge with Paul watching over them. We felt we needed someone to protect them, as the most dangerous time is when an entity is being forcefully removed from our world. They will use any means they can to try to ensure they remain firmly implanted in our world, including frightening people or children or trying to latch onto them. By placing Paul with them, he would be able to hold them in a protective circle and keep them safe. While we were walking around upstairs and trying to determine where we need to start, Paul and Stuart had been generally chatting together. We had decided that the children's room was to be our starting point. Kelly began by saying there was something wrong with the adjoining wall through the properties. She could feel a dark presence on the other side of the wall and it appeared to be trying to enter the room we were standing in. Paul called up the stairs and asked to have a word. It would seem the neighbours either side of the property had been using a type of the Ouija board. Directly behind the house was a cemetery, and the neighbours to the left were convinced that through the board they had been communicating with people in the cemetery. The people on the right had also been talking to numerous people, yet things had turned rather nasty there and on one occasion the female of the house had been thrown against the wall and pinned in mid-air for several seconds by some unseen force. He went on to say a few doors down another couple were having problems and they were trying to move to get away from it.

The other side work in mysterious ways, and by placing Paul downstairs we had gained vital information, information which Stuart had not offered to any of us on arrival. But at least we now knew the entry point. Again, it would seem that we had an energy line running directly through these properties, and these entities, kindly invited in by the adjoining neighbours, had been tormenting this young family.

The children's room appeared so dark, despite being painted in beautiful bright blues, yellows and reds. Even the brand-new carpet which lay under our feet had a feeling of uncleanliness. It soon was clear that the little girl was no little girl at all, this was indeed a dark, sinister black figure. Its accomplice appeared to be like a black centipede, that was the least four feet in length, yet when it was pinned down, shrank into a tiny ball. Sinister red eyes still shone out, throwing darkness in fear around the room. It was to become apparent later that Janine wasn't really a true believer and had only agreed to our visit in a desperate attempt to try and help the children. But she herself that night witnessed the power that dark entity brought with it and she felt its presence being ripped from the house. Within moments of us beginning to concentrate our energy, as we tuned in, I turned to Janine and said, 'Whatever is here in this room disturbs anyone who sleeps in here, it tries to keep people away at night and this is why the children wake-up terrified.' I could feel it dancing in the darkness and waiting for the innocent victims to fall asleep so it could attack. Janine went on to tell us that when they first moved in the house, they had all slept in this room and neither her or her partner had ever had a decent night's sleep. In fact, they had both suffered nightmares when they slept in this room and the children often had nightmares since moving in this house.

I physically saw it climb onto Lyn and enter into her aura. You could see a dark shadow descend across the face, large dark circles appeared under her eyes and a six o'clock shadow spread across her face. You could see the sneer beginning to form. While fully in control she allowed this being to enter into her aura. She knew she had the power to overcome this disembodied spirit. The entity on the other hand was so desperate to be in the human body, it immediately took up the challenge of this open, inviting aura, without ever stopping to consider the consequences of its actions. Lyn held her vibration as still as she possibly could, while this entity moved in and began to try to throw influence over her body. Lyn held her own arms behind her own back, to ensure this entity did not try to attack me. She then slowly raised her head and looked directly into my eyes. Momentarily I averted my eyes, the purpose being to lure this disembodied spirit into thinking it had control over its body and that we were incapable of dealing with it. I carefully read the signs from Lyn. All it took was for one nod of the head for me to realise she now had the spirit held fully within her body. All Kevin and I had to do now is to collectively build up enough power to push it through the other side. So together we worked as one with our guides and began to push this entity through a darkened doorway back to its own world. We pushed, it clung. Then with one final push, Lyn spiked her energy to throw it off, and at the same time pulling every inch of power in we could, we gave an almighty push. As we did so, Lyn physically fell back, barely managing to grab her footing at the force of this entity being knocked by us and pulled by the other side back to where it belonged.

We waited a few moments for Lyn to gain her balance and to get back control of her own body. We then began to search the room and see what else was there. Both Linda, Kevin and I were drawn back to the adjoining wall. We could feel something moving backwards and forwards, bricks and mortar are no boundary to this dark entity. Kevin was the first one to speak, he said, 'I know you will think I'm crazy, but this looks like a long black centipede.'

Quick as a flash Lyn added, 'No, we don't think you're crazy at all, we have come across one of these before. Don't let it anywhere near and stay out of the way,' she said rather forcefully.

"Don't worry, I won't,' he added, with a smile spreading across his face. Lyn and I had indeed come across this type of dark entity before. We had seen what it could do when it had possessed a young lad. Quick as a flash, between us we built a tunnel of light around it, ensuring it could come nowhere near us. We then opened a further doorway and began to push it through. For some reason it needed very little persuasion; we had removed its accomplice and there seemed very little reason for it to stay. Yet we still provided the earthly energy and power to help it on its way. This allowed the other side to do their work. Kevin went on to describe how he could see this black mass, slowly slipping and sliding through the Gateway.

'Oh, my goodness,' Janine said, 'I can feel something on me, I feel funny, kind of tingling, I'm not sure what is happening.'

'Don't worry,' I said, 'it is just the remnants of this dark force and the energies associated with it leaving the room.' At the same time, I looked across at her reassuringly and smiled and so did the others. You could feel her nervousness, yet she had no choice but to believe us, as this was going on around her and at this moment in time, there was nothing else she could do.

Slowly the sensation began to leave her. I could sense things were getting better around her and I turned to her and said, "Are you okay?"

'I'm much better thank you,' she said. You could feel from the vibration that she was much more at ease than before, and whatever had been bothering her had long gone. Janine turned to us all and said, 'My goodness, doesn't it look brighter in here, or is it my imagination?'

'No, it is not,' I added. Dark entities overlay a dark energy whenever they reside. When they are removed the darkness goes with them. Most of the time we don't notice that the room was dark, it is only when it becomes light, we realise just how dark the place was.

We then began to work on changing the energy in the room and by building wall upon wall of impenetrable energy between the adjoining walls in both bedrooms. Knowing we had a problem on the other side, we also built protective walls on that side as well. We extended them into the loft and eighteen feet above the house and eighteen feet below to try to ensure that nothing could penetrate through.

Once we had finished the children's bedroom we went into Janine and Stuart's bedroom. While there was no entity here there was still a shadow of darkness and an aftermath left from the presence of these dark vibrations.

The next thing we did was to go down into the lounge. We all thought our troubles were over and we had finished our work. It soon became clear that this was not the case and there were equally dark vibrations in this room, and indeed another entity. Janine went upstairs with the children, while we kept Stuart with us. It soon became apparent that Stuart was by far a greater non-believer than Janine. That was until he felt something jump on him; he became unbalanced and momentarily developed double vision. This unseen entity had jumped onto his back and this is what you could feel. Not wishing to scare him, we quietly began working in unison, in the process of ridding him of this uninvited invasion.

Fortunately for us this dark figure had had very little opportunity to embed itself into his auric field before we began the onslaught of dragging it off. In moments we had got him, and with the work of our spirit guides he was ensconced back where he belonged. We repeated the process from upstairs and ensured the walls were impenetrable from either side.

Happy our work was done, we chatted for a little while, offering advice to them both. You could see they were both shocked by what they had witnessed that night. I advised them to tell both neighbours, as it may not be called a Ouija board, but whatever it may be, it was equally as dangerous and they should dispose of it as soon as possible. I also offered my telephone number and told them both to tell the neighbours if they needed any help, just to give me a call.

I didn't hear from them, but then again, I didn't expect to. To ask for the telephone number would be like admittance that they had caused problems in the neighbour's house. So it would seem they would continue to suffer in silence. Hopefully we would never hear from Stuart or Janine again and we had built up enough energy between the properties to keep out whatever those neighbours chose to call in.

The Pretender

In three years, Joanne had suffered more pain than most people face in a lifetime. Her mother had died suddenly, and she had lost a baby girl seven months into the pregnancy. But the most painful experience had been the death of her little boy. His short life ended when a drunk driver mounted the pavement outside of their home. Stephen never stood a chance, at six years old he lost his life. He lived for a short period of time, and all his mother could do was helplessly look on while the life ebbed away from him. Here she was four years on, she was, quite rightly, still grieving his death.

Joanne and Dave had lived in the same house all their married life. The house had been in the family and had been built in the 1940s. Recently there had been a flurry of activity in the house. Most of the activity appeared to focus on Joanne, although her son, who was in his early twenties, and her husband did not get off scot-free. The extent to which the son was being bombarded would only come to light as the evening unfolded.

There did not appear to be one single event or episode that prompted Joanne to contact me. It seemed that she just woke up one morning and decided she had

had enough. For years she had tolerated doors slamming upstairs when she was down and downstairs when she was up. People running up and down the stairs with such vigour the house trembled, this would last for several minutes. It did not confine itself to when Joanne was in, the neighbours reported hearing it when she was out, as if loads of people were thundering up and down the stairs. The neighbours became concerned her eldest son had friends in while mom was out, and they were causing damage. They were a little perturbed to find no one was in the house at the time, it was merely unseen beings creating the din. Joanne felt for a while they didn't actually believe her. Windows would fly open on their own accord and she had returned from work on more than one occasion to find her lounge window wide open. Both her and Dave were at a loss to understand why and how this had happened. Joanne often felt something was watching her, especially when she was in the kitchen. She constantly felt uncomfortable in her own home and could not settle. Through a friend of a friend, she had obtained my telephone number. After talking to Joanne for about five minutes it was very clear she had a real problem in her house. In detail Joanne had explained all the physical events that had occurred. She added that possibly the worst situation was the mood of the house. It always seemed heavy and suppressive. Arguments amongst the three of them appeared to be a regular occurrence, and most the time there seemed to be no reason why people were arguing, they just did.

I agreed to arrange to come and see as soon as I could get a team together. Very hesitantly Joanne asked if our actions would remove all spirits from the house, good and bad. She went on to explain her son came to see her on a regular basis and she was terrified we would banish her dead son in the process. I assured her we wouldn't. Both ourselves and our etheric helpers could tell the difference between good and bad. Besides, her son would no doubt stay out of the way for the cleansing, so he would be perfectly safe. I had to give her further reassurance on the night we arrived that nothing was going to stop her deceased son from popping in to see her from time to time.

Paul, Lyn Patrick and myself all converged outside the house. Once inside we spent just a few minutes exchanging pleasantries before we began to check and scan the house to see if there was anything untoward within the four walls. Confident the problem appeared to be on the upper floor, we made our way upstairs and slowly walked around the rooms. As soon as we entered into the rear bedroom, we knew we had found the problem, now all that was required was a solution. The room itself appeared dark, the wallpaper, duvet cover and curtains did nothing to lift the dark dank, foreboding feeling that you had as soon as you entered this room. You could feel the anger. Whatever ethereal entity that resided in this room brought with them a dark, suppressive feeling. As soon as we entered the room, we immediately sealed it; now whatever was in here was trapped. As we did so, I was convinced I felt a further entity join us through the adjoining property wall. I could feel this entity as it bounced around the room. I began to open a link between myself and this being and began to communicate with it, while trying to hold it at a distance to ensure I did not become one of his victims and violent. I began to describe him, as I spoke, I could feel my face writhing and contorting with this black dark rage, which had engulfed this man for the majority of his life. A dark emotion so out of control it had to have a vent. What made the situation worse, was it was further fired by booze, yet each weekend he consumed this harmful potion by the bucket load. As I tuned in, I relayed this back to the group. I spoke of the annoyance I felt towards my wife, the useless kid. Joanne watched with intent. She then went on to say this was the precise behaviour of her former neighbour. He was a wife and child beater, a drunk who came home intoxicated with alcohol most weekends. Fired by this fuel, rows would pursue into the early hours of the next day, invariably only stopping when the Police arrived. It would seem they had separated, and this man had sadly passed to spirit twelve years previously. So here he was. A neighbour who had shifted and was now the entity tormenting Joanne and her family.

Not so, here we had a victim. I wonder if this man had really been this angry or had something else been tormenting him? Something which had taken over his life and something he was unable to distinguish from himself. I believed he too was a victim. They said the spirit had never been like this before. Hot-headed yes, but not violent. It would seem he had made the mistake, on his demise, of returning to his former abode. Now he was trapped and held here. He had burst through the wall seconds before we sealed it, trapping him on the other side. Now he was here, and we knew of him. It would have been quite easy for us to believe this was the root cause of the problem. It wasn't. Here was something that was just as much a victim as the people of the house. The captor just sat back nestled down in the corner, safe in the knowledge we would focus our attentions on this lost soul and the darkness would remain undetected. Between us we quickly and proficiently opened the doors of his jail and sent him on his way. Now we had to contend with this entity.

We could sense him in the far corner, not necessarily hiding, but sitting, motionless, watching us. This was something not of our world, a concentration of dark, foreboding energy. It felt like the weight of a rock, yet in a semi-solid form, it could shift and move. It was a living energy, a powerpack which radiated out an array of emotion provoking energies. All negative. It could create strands of jealousy, resentment or hatred, which it radiated out at any unsuspecting human it could find. They inadvertently absorbed them, assuming them as their own. These droplets would expand by a thousand percent. Now it would harvest its crop and absorb it through its vibration, growing stronger all the time.

'Okay, guys, what do we have here? And if we do, where is it?' I asked, directing the question at them all.

Patrick was quick to respond. 'There is something horrible in here, I feel like it is trying to attack my throat, I can hardly breathe, it is like some sort of darkness,' he added. You could see he was uncomfortable, he began to move around the room. At the same time, he began to try and loosen the clothing around his neck.

Lyn saw, sensed and felt and was always one of the last ones to say anything, analysing what the others said, ensuring she was comfortable with her own findings before she spoke. I looked at her and she looked at me. She pointed into the same corner I had been pulled to earlier. 'Black, red eyes, about three feet tall, crouched up in the corner over there,' she said, gesturing her hand without really looking to where she was pointing. I turned to Paul, no need for words, he just nodded in the same direction and so did Patrick. So we knew what was here, now we needed to understand why. We began to scan the land. You could feel the importance of this area. Water lay under this house, this was the conduit, several energy lines ran through it, this was the means of travel. Joanne told us an old Priory had lay to the left some distance down the road, although no one really knew its true location. I felt this information was slightly off the mark. It didn't lie to the north, I believed, or I was shown, it actually lay to the northwest.

Unfortunately for Joanne it lay directly onto the energy line which coursed through her house. This was the original source of contamination. Violent death had been the fall of many of the monasteries and this one felt no different. This black mass of energy felt part of this terrible period. This belonged to a far greater source of destruction, which lay on the other side of the doorway. Its missionaries, soldiers of darkness, did their evil work, creating fear and dark energies, then harvesting them to feed themselves, then sending the remainder of the energy back to the father of them all. I couldn't see what it was, just a huge black mass, so dense and dark, no form could be made out. It didn't matter, it could not reach us, other than through its minions, and we could not reach it. It was safely ensconced in its own dark world.

We knew what we had, so now we began to tune in and feel its power. It was similar to what had happened to the man next door, but on this occasion, it was the teenage son who was the victim. 'Have you been having problems with attitude from your son?' I asked.

'Hah! And some!' she added.

'Is he rude, mouthy, disrespectful and prone to massive temper tantrums?' I said.

'Do you know him?' she asked sarcastically.

No, I didn't know him, but I could feel what this entity was like, and I could feel his energy throughout the room. Traces of negativity hung in the air, clinging to the very fabric of the room and the powerpack was the dark, red-eyed beast pinned in the corner of the room.

Collectively we joined our minds together and began to work as one. With the help of our guides we began to box this entity in and push it through the other side. In the first instance it came back at us, generating a huge force of darkness which it threw at us. Its focus was Joanne. It knew if it could hurt her, it would be game over. Immediately I gave the instruction to Joanne, not to look into the corner. In seconds Paul moved in front of her creating a human shield, he could take the onslaught. The dark vibration penetrating his auric field like slithers of glass. Paul could withstand it, we would cleanse him later. In the meantime, our aim was to get this beast out of this house and back to its own world. For about ten minutes we battled, light against the dark, until eventually it began to weaken. The battle was over, we had bombarded it with light. Much more light, than the dark it could generate. You felt it began to lose its hold. In a huge, concerted effort we pushed it over the other side and shut and sealed the door. We then exchanged the energy in the room, replacing it will a much softer, calmer energy. This we repeated across the top floor and then made our way downstairs.

As we stood in the lounge looking through to the kitchen it was as if we were looking up an incline. It was as if no walls existed and you could see the flow of dark energy moving in the direction of the former monastery.

It seemed like clouds of darkness moving along this imaginary road. We needed to clear the energy from the underside of the house, to purify the stagnant water. This was our first task. Using waves and columns of light, we began to dissipate the darkness from the underside of the house. Once we were happy the pool of water was free of dark energies we began to focus on the line, we needed to divert it around the house. So together we began to push the energy to the left, so it ran in-between to the two houses.

After ninety minutes we had cleared out this dark demon, cleansed and replaced the energy throughout the property and shifted the energy line. This was the most important one, to ensure the negative vortex of the former monastery and Joanne's house were in no way connected, and we had achieved this.

Why was I not surprised to receive a phone call from Joanne? As we had sat in the pub reflecting, I had said to the others that Joanne's Achilles heel was her son and her fear of never feeling him around her again. If this Demon was to take on the form of her son, then all would be lost and we would be back. Lyn felt sure that was the case and we had a friendly bet. Lyn was convinced we would be back within a month. She was right. I had the telephone call after two weeks and a week later we were back in the house.

Joanne had explained that shortly after we had gone, she kept getting the feeling her son had been sent over at the same him. She was convinced he was trapped and was calling her for help. The communicator was not her son, it was the minion for the darkness, pretending to be her son. This demon had been on to a good thing and was determined to try and find a way back in. It had impressed upon Joanne that it was her son and it was trapped. It called upon her to try and help. Call me and I can come back, it pleaded, and Joanne believed him. In truth it was only a half belief, but the gamble was too great, she could not afford to take the risk. Within days it was back and with a vengeance. This time it seemed worse than before. Now her son was terrified, and her husband was completely freaked by it. Two cut-glass brandy glasses had flown out of the wall unit with such force and landed right side up on a small coffee table on the opposite side of the room. What made the situation more difficult to understand was the fact the doors on the wall unit remained completely shut. The running up and down the stairs got ten times worse.

When we arrived Joanne apologised, she knew she had inadvertently brought this thing back in. In truth any mother would have done the same. So we started working on it all over again. There it was back in the corner of the room the same as before, sitting on the corner of the double bed, half on top and half of this demon actually through the bed, as if transposed on it. This time it did not have enough power to do battle with us. Before it had been well established. A parasite who had lived off many different humans, thus making it extremely powerful. This time it had nothing but the evil it had brought with it. Most of that had been expended terrifying the family. As a result, it was no match for us, within a few minutes it was safely ensconced back where it belonged, in the bowels of hell.

Before I left, I sat and talked to both Joanne and Dave. I brought their dead son through to then. I gave them memory after memory for about fifteen minutes, until they knew, without doubt, I was talking to Stephen. I could hear his giggles and feel the warmth of his personality. Afterwards I explained he hadn't gone anywhere and here I was happily conversing with him, long after the dark beast had been removed. I reassured her Stephen would always be around her, whenever she needed him. He would never miss a special occasion, like a birthday, so she was not to worry. I also told her Stephen would not be calling her begging for help. He didn't need help, he was safely growing up on the other side in the care of her mother and her grandmother, and every time he came, they would bring him to ensure he got here safely. Did she understand? But more importantly, did she believe me? And just to make the point, I gave her messages from both her nan and her mom. That was what she needed, Joanne reassured me she did believe, and in her heart she knew he would never be calling her, merely visiting her instead and making his presence known.

We all knew it was over and our services would never be required here again. We had finally cut off its only doorway back, through a mother's love. We left in the knowledge we had beaten it and if it wished to return, it would have to find another victim. Unfortunately, no doubt it would.

The Shadow People

Sue had never considered that the issues with her very young daughter may be related to something unearthly's intervention. She had put down her daughter's inability to sleep at night and insistence on being in her parents' bed as wilful behaviour. It took an awful long time for her to realise this was not the case. The situation was further compounded by the fact Taylor had also been reluctant to go in her own bed. Like most young children she preferred the comfort of her parents' room. In their new home a compromise had been achieved. Taylor was now sleeping on the floor on an inflatable mattress. Even then she was continuing to moan, preferring to be in the bed and on the side now occupied by her father. He had point blank refused to sleep in the spare room for even one more night.

Sue had been very slow to realise something was amiss. She had rationalised the whole process. The freezing cold energy which seemed to envelope Taylor's room, the rotting fetid smells; electrics which would blow, power supplies cut off. The rabbit's frequent bouts of thumping the floor. The darkness that encased the kitchen, and finally the terrible fire which had resulted in the house being gutted. When you put it all together, it made sense. Sue's partner was away for a few days when it hit her. There was something in their house and something was amiss. Coincidentally, and as Sue was a friend, we were able to visit that night. So a hastily assembled gang harmonised their energies together before engaging in battle with the dark forces in this house.

Following the fire, the property had been refurbished from top to bottom two years ago. There was no poorly maintained property here, everything was immaculate. Yet at the same time pockets of darkness hid in corners, casting odd shadows across the rooms.

We walked and paced throughout the ground floor of the house. We were all in agreement the worst of the energies clung to the long, narrow galley kitchen and dining area. 'What sits above here?' I enquired.

'Taylor's bedroom and part of our room.' We looked at each other and began to exchange knowing smiles. 'Please don't tell me there really is something disturbing her, I shall feel terrible'. It would seem Sue would have to feel terrible, there was something in this house. In fact, more than one thing.

We decided that while there was a problem in mom's room, the main area we needed to worry about was in Taylor's room. With the room sealed we began to tune in and try to establish contact with whatever was here. I could feel alcohol and the need to consume vast quantities of it. I could feel the urge growing by the minute. This entity ran through each and every one of us, trying to find a weakness and foothold in order to attach itself. This entity was trying to get away from something, it was desperate. It was held in some strange vibrational force and was looking for a way out. It sensed the end was near. It knew we had detected him and now he was out to break free from whatever held him here. As he bounced off our auras, we all complained of different sensations. Headaches, chest pain, stomach ache, such was the force this entity hit us with. This entity was a coward. He had managed to avoid detection by preying on this little girl. He fed on her fear and through his behaviours, he created more fear, to the point the little girl was terrified to go into her room. When she did, he woke her up and terrified her. We saw all this for ourselves. We watched the shadows dance around the top of the walls, creating frightening images and faces, that seemed to traverse down the walls as if in search of her. They made no impact on us at all. It merely increased our intent to remove this disembodied entity back where it belonged. Powered by the hidden force, it continued its repertoire. It faded in and out. Growing huge, then shrinking back. It came right up to our faces, as if it was about to try and engulf, then disappeared to nothing. For several minutes it kept up its performance. This entity was of human form, yet over the years it had clearly become more adept at practising these terrifying performances.

We decided we had seen enough. There was no escaping from us. His time to leave this world had come and gone long ago. His attachment to alcohol held him here. Now he was going to be removed back to the other side. He gave a half-hearted attempt to avoid his fate. In reality he knew resistance was futile and in a few short moments he would be gone.

He was not our problem, our issue was the Shadow People. Shadow People are believed to belong to armies of the dead, disembodied spirits that reside within the underworld. Some believe they form armies, fighting for the demons who rule the underworld, their foot soldiers serving the darkness. Once released into our world, they work in unison together, moving quickly, wreaking chaos wherever they go. While the man may have been bothering Sue's daughter, it was these Shadow People who were tormenting her.

Together we worked on inviting these Shadow People in the room, watching patiently as they entered the room dancing across the walls. We were all conscious of the risk we exposed ourselves, vulnerable as we allowed these dark entities to get so close to us. Within minutes they were all in the room, running across the walls, the ceilings, dancing across our auric fields as if toying with us. Once in we shot into action, sealing the room and quickly opening a dark doorway back to the underworld from where they came. Within minutes we had pushed each and every one of them through the door. As quickly as we opened it, we sealed it. We then began to clear the room of the negativity and replace it with a warmer, kinder energy.

Soon the place was clear and these entities never came back. We never discovered who had let these beings in. We certainly cleared the space and within a few days Taylor was happily playing in her room and sleeping in there again. In the early days she occasionally spoke to her mom about it, explaining that she hadn't wanted to worry her or upset her, so she had kept quiet.

The Witch's Bottle

Several years ago, I had been to Gemma's house, close
to the village of Coven, which in itself seems a bit of a
giveaway. Yet for years I had never associated the name
with witches. It was also something the local
community were keen to do, disassociate their name
from connections with the occult.

At the time of my previous visit Gemma had been
in the early stages of her pregnancy. Richard was now
three years old. She explained she had just been through
a rather messy divorce. The house had been filled with
arguments and negative energy. She had now moved on
and in fact had met someone else. Gemma believed the
house was not happy and she felt a presence in several
of the rooms. Richard, her little boy, was sleeping quite
poorly and talking of monsters that visited him in the
night. A black presence was seen moving in and out of
Gemma's bedroom and the house felt awful.

I still sometimes find it difficult to understand how
people manage to live with the things they do. Or how
they manage to forget a lot of the information
surrounding a haunting. But they do and Gemma was no
exception. Listening to Gemma's account of events, the
situation did not appear to seem too bad. Yet when we

pressed her for information it soon became apparent the problem was much worse than we first thought. I was glad I had followed my instinct and come with a team of four rather than the two I would use when I think it is not too bad.

As I often do, I had asked for Gemma to remove her son from the house at the time of the clearance. When we arrived at Gemma's, her partner was running a little late and had not arrived yet. He was going to take Richard and the dog out for a short period of time. We had chatted idly while we waited and Gemma expressed her concern that a lot of activity appeared to be around the child's room.

As we had pulled up in the car, Richard was fast asleep on the sofa. As we approached the house he had sprung onto his feet and was running round the room wildly, saying no, no. This had really unnerved Gemma. I suddenly decided to do a U-turn as Craig arrived to take Richard out. I felt I had to talk to the child and find out what was happening. Why was a lot of the activity focused around him? Why was he distressed by our presence? I felt we needed to get to the bottom of this. So all plans were changed and now Craig was in the thick of it and looking decidedly uncomfortable.

We all sat together in the small living room making small chit chat. Richard was clearly very tired and sat cuddling Gemma, looking like he was about to fall asleep. I turned my attention to Richard and asked him outright why I was there with my friends? 'Because of the monsters,' he replied, burying his face into his mother's cardigan. It seemed he wanted to talk to me but appeared afraid to do so.

'Who told you I was coming?' I queried.

'Monsters,' came the reply.

A puzzled Gemma asked the question herself. 'Monsters? Do they talk to you?' she asked.

'Yes,' he replied.

'Where are they now?'

Before I had finished talking, his arm stretched out and pointed upwards, and at the same time a muffled reply clearly said, 'My bedroom, in the cupboard.' A knowing look came across Gemma's face. I gave a gentle shake of my head, outside of Richards vision. We could talk about it once we were away from little ears. I made a snap decision to keep Richard and Craig downstairs with Patrick, who would stand guard over them both. I promised Richard I would not go until all the monsters had left the house. His trusting eyes locked onto mine and I knew he believed me, and I knew I would keep my promise. Two hours later a very tired group left that house and we had kept our promise.

We left the three of them in the front room and moved into the other lounge. We shut the door firmly behind us. If we talked too loud, Patrick would warn us. So we began to explore the rest of the downstairs of the house. The wood burner was running on full, yet the room was freezing cold. I pulled my coat tighter, as did the others. No need for words, without any spoken words Gemma told us the house was always cold. The fire could be fully on and sometimes you could see your breath when standing a few feet away from it. All the time we had chatted to Richard I had scratched my head, it felt as it something was gently jabbing at the whole of my head, causing a real irritation. I explained the sensation, which Lyn was clearly feeling, as I watched her scratch too. Gemma explained this happened to her during the night and she would wake up with piles of hair on the pillow. This only happened when she was here. Until recently she had had very long hair, but due to the amount she had lost she had recently had it cut off to her shoulders. Yet the problem still continued. This stayed with me for the whole of the evening and only stopped when the last unearthly occupant was pushed through the doorway.

Throughout the house there was a continual blast of cold energy, as if we were standing in an open gully and air was being forced through a narrow opening causing a distinct breeze to waft past us. This could be felt in the second lounge, kitchen and in complete alignment on the upper floors. Later as we stood on the long landing which led to the bathroom, we watched the cord from the bathroom light gently swaying in the breeze. On the end of the cord was a weighted ceramic knob, yet the cord still swayed. Gemma explained sometimes it was so severe the knob banged against the wall. During the night this could last for several hours, stopping when she looked at it, only to start again as she turned away.

The house was over three floors. Two bedrooms were on the middle floor and Richard's bedroom was on the top floor. We entered the second bedroom in between Gemma's room and the bathroom. It was horrid, the room was painted black. We looked at each other. Gemma confided that her ex-partner had been growing cannabis in this room, he had been arrested and the plants removed. She thought this may be the reason. All three of us shook our heads, no it wasn't the cause, but the anger and shame over this had added to the negativity within the house. We did not feel the presence was here, just a build-up of energies which we could deal with later. We found the same with the bathroom and Gemma's room, no presence just a heavy, dark, dank atmosphere.

We climbed the narrow stairs to Richard's bedroom. You could feel it in this room, there was definitely something here. It was smart, sinister and intelligent, it knew we were after it and it was not going to make our life any easier. This room was massive, a bedroom at one end and a play area at the other. There was built-in furniture, lots and lots of toys and a door leading up to the attic. Psychically I was shown a vessel, like a genie in a bottle. I turned to Gemma and asked her if she had found something in the last few months and brought it in the house? She pondered my question, shaking her head slowly from side to side, then in a light bulb moment stated they had been walking over the heath recently and had found a green glass bottle. She went and showed it to us. I knew immediately whatever was bothering them here was attached to this. They had inadvertently brought a Demon into their home. We would dispose of this as we left. In the meantime, we needed to deal with this issue.

As we scanned the room, I heard Patrick calling me. I moved out of the room to the small landing at the top of the stairs. Patrick informed me Richard had stopped playing with his toys and told Patrick the monster was hiding in the attic. How did he know we were struggling? I don't know, but his intervention changed things for us.

We clambered up to the attic and there it was sitting on the ceiling joist tucked up in the corner out of sight. Between the three of us we were able to grab it, net it and move it on. We gave it the opportunity to leave of its own accord and return to the field and the land. It merely flew at us, trying to overpower us. The irritation in my head grew worse and developed into pains, I refused to acknowledge the entity, and after a bit of a battle we managed to capture it, open a gateway and return it to the world from where it came.

We moved through the floors, systematically cleaning as we went. I gave Gemma the glass bottle, she went to the bottom of the garden and threw it with all her might over to the scrubland behind the house.

We returned to the living room. Gemma asked Richard if he was okay. He nodded, and without looking up from his cars, said that the monster was gone now.

Then he raised his head and gave his mom an amazing smile. Lyn looked and me and said, 'Well that is good enough proof for me.' I think we all felt a sense of contentment by this small statement.

Gemma rang me a few days later to say everything was calm at the house and Richard was much happier, he then never mentioned the monsters again.

I suppose the message here is to be very careful taking home something you find. You may end up with more than you wished for.

Where is the Water Coming From?

I wasn't the first person to visit Duna's home, but hopefully I would be the last. Duna lived in a first-floor flat in a quiet suburb with her three children, aged four, six and seven years old. The apartment had three bedrooms and was quite a spacious and modern flat. Yet the children were terrified to go into their own rooms. All three of them complained of seeing a shadow in their room looking over them. The flat was often filled with obnoxious smells and the cause could not be identified. A strange mist was seen in several of the rooms. Items would fly off the work units in the kitchen. Pools of water appeared from nowhere on the floors in the kitchen, bathroom and hallway. Duna complained of a sensation of being watched wherever she went in the flat. If that was not bad enough, there was the sensation of a pressure, as if someone was lying on top of her when she was in bed.

The whole family had resorted to sleeping in the lounge and by the time we visited they had been doing this for several months.

We were to discover later that no one in the block of six flats had been free from these ghostly apparitions. All had been subjected to physic phenomena and attack from disembodied fiends.

When Paul, Patrick, Lyn and I arrived, Duna was waiting for us outside the block, with her ex-partner the father to her children. You could feel his unease at the whole situation. It transpired he didn't believe in any of this 'bullshit', yet the love of his children and their welfare drove him on. This was the sole reason he came that night.

From the outside the block felt like any normal block of flats. There was nothing to indicate what was waiting for us inside. As soon as we began to climb the stairs a feeling of dirt and oppression began to envelop us all.

The flat felt dark, tired, cold and unkempt. Even in the children's bedroom, there was nothing that felt warm or inviting. As we walked slowly around the flat there was a feeling as if the walls were closing in on you. Something was always standing behind you, watching you as you walked from room to room. But always out of sight.

The smell of stagnant water, mould and damp in the children's room was overpowering, yet there was no sign of damp in flat.

The kitchen and hallway floors were covered in laminate flooring. As I walked across the room in the kitchen, my foot began to slide across the floor, as if a pool of water lay on the floor.

The dark lighting throughout the flat made it almost impossible to see. Yet on inspection the floor was dry.

Everywhere I stepped my shoes slid across the floor in the same action. Duna explained pools of water had been discovered with no apparent source. As I moved around the kitchen and the hallway, I was having difficulty walking as my feet constantly slipped from underneath me on the imaginary water.

Finally, we went into the bathroom. All four of us felt drawn to this room, as tiny as it was, we all filed in with Duna and Mick, the ex, standing close by in the hallway. As we tuned in together, I felt the presence of a man. Immediately, with my third eye I saw the events unfold in front of my eyes. Hanging limply from the pipework above the shower by a noose, which was tightly wrapped around his neck, hung the body of a man in his late forties or early fifties, unkempt clothes, facial stubble and bulging eyes stared blankly ahead.

I disengaged for a moment and turned to Duna and asked if she knew much about the history of the flat. 'I know a man committed suicide in here,' she said. She then added, 'I think its him who is haunting us.' I tilted my head on one side as if to say maybe, but I was not convinced.

I began to describe the man to her. 'This man was in late forties or early fifties, around five feet seven inches tall' I said.

'That's him,' she said, amazed I had been able to describe this main so accurately.

'He is not the problem,' Patrick said. I nodded in agreement. I wondered how much this resident evil had in fact contributed to this man's death. I could only speculate. We knew where this man was and we would deal with him later.

There seemed to be numerous entities occupying this flat. There seemed to be 'a darkness', a dark, thick vibration, without form. This was the centre of the activity in this flat. A huge, black cloud of negativity, yet it was more than this. It was an intelligent form, which had the ability to sense our weaknesses and then play on them. It searched each and every one of us, looking for some weakness it could use for its own end.

Suddenly without warning I found myself suffering from an asthma attack, I had not experienced anything like this in a long time and there was no reason for this. As the minutes ticked on Paul became unnerved by the foreboding presence that surrounded the house. Lyn became agitated by the lack of progress and Patrick was without direction. It knew precisely what it was doing.

This thing was the root cause of all these events. The cause of the slippery floor, the obnoxious smell. It was the controlling force that created these events. It negatively influenced everything it came into contact with and was determined to carry on doing so.

We decided the best place to begin the clearance was in the lounge. While this appeared to be the least affected of the whole flat, it was big and spacious, so we could keep Mick and Duna with us.

We reinforced the walls of the rooms and built a doorway across the hall to limit what could come in at one time, to avoid being overcome by this presence. We carefully planted Mick and Duna in-between. Then we opened a darkened doorway to the side of Lyn. We would use her aura to pull them through.

I commanded that no more than two beings be allowed through at one time.

With everything in place, we began to clear this flat of this evil force. As we began, I felt the presence of the suicide victim from the bathroom, you could feel him being channelled through a narrow corridor, created by the 'other side'. This entity was herded through this curved subway which ended alongside Lyn. This was a one-way passageway and as soon as he entered the room, the tunnel disintegrated before us. Lyn stood silently offering her aura as a warm enticing zone. Once he became entangled here there was no way out.

Within seconds he moved towards Lyn. We had Duna's permission to shift him on with or without his co-operation. I was just about to begin the banishment, when he stopped and made one last plea. He wished to apologise to Duna for frightening her children. He never meant to do this. It would seem he too was a victim controlled and forced to do things against his will by the black fiend. I turned to Duna and told her what he was saying. No words were spoken, she merely nodded and said thank you. This was all he needed to release him from this hell hole — her forgiveness and the knowledge that she knew he had never intended and would never have hurt her children. He was now free. He needed no help to leave our world and without any prompting, he sought the doorway himself and stepped through without a backward glance.

As soon as we were sure he was clear, the doorway closed. Simultaneously the passageway of light re-opened and the next perpetrator walked the tunnel. I immediately sensed two people this time. 'How many people are here, Lyn?' I asked.

'Two,' she mouthed, as she held up a hand showing two digits. This had never happened before, but I was comfortable that at least Lyn knew she had two entities to deal with. There was a blond female, stout, unkempt, in her early forties. Alongside her stood a man, slightly built and of a similar age and in a similar condition. I tuned in. I knew these people had led similar lives. I saw the smoking, drinking and debauchery. I could see cannabis being smoked in a room dense with smoke. I could feel the atmosphere, violent, sinister and uncaring. Everyone fuelled by alcohol. I felt the pain to my right side. A violent kick to my head. The man was showing me how he exited this plane. Then a further kick, followed by more and more blows, as the other joined in this vicious onslaught. I fall to the ground, abandoned, unable to move due to my injuries and inebriated state. I choke and drown on my own blood. This was the end to this man's life. He felt able to leave after showing us what had happened to him. He was the mist that appeared in nearly every room, the eyes that watched Duna. With very little effort he too went through the doorway.

The female was different. She had nothing to share and was going nowhere. We gave her no chance to escape. We held her in Lyn's vibration and slowly unpeeled her and pushed her through the opening.

Next came a little girl, or was it a female? It was difficult to determine. That was enough for me. Here we had the resident evil, the source of power, the cause of the misery. The jailor and controller. It started to grow and grow in size and began to spin. I saw a shield form across my eyes and an urgent voice: 'Do not look.' I turned to the others and very calmly said, 'Do not look at this entity, do not look in this direction. Keep your eyes diverted to the floor until I tell you otherwise.' You could feel the power swept around the room with every rotation this being made. It was creating a diversion, something for us to look at. Then it would have us. We would move from 'clearer' to victim. In unison Patrick, Lyn, Paul and I gave it all we had got, and we pushed it through the door. With eyes averted we poured as much power as we could muster to knock this beast through the doorway. As soon as we had part of it in the door, I felt a huge force rip this thing through. As it did, instantaneously we had a parade of animals enter into the room, although their doorway was much brighter and kinder. An old, brown-and-white boxer dog had a muzzle which was much too tight to be removed as it limped across the doorway. Abused chickens flew through the doorway screeching in fear, other dogs, cats and farm animals made the procession through towards freedom and the light. They too had been captive in this evil wave.

Finally, a huge Jamaican man stepped in. In unison we all described him, he seemed to have to duck to exit the tunnel. He towered over Lyn. He almost apologised for being here. He was like a gentle giant, yet he too had been held in this evil vibration. He did not appear to be able to believe his luck: he was free yet bedazzled by the speed in which things had happened. As soon as he walked in, you could see him looking around, weighing up the situation and looking for a way out. He spotted the open doorway and skipped through. In a moment he was gone. The whole process from start to finish had taken twenty minutes. We were physically exhausted by it all. The flat began to feel better, although patches of darkness held in the corners of the room, still silently and patiently waiting for the chance to pull the evil blanket back into our world. We searched every room led by our Guides, looking for minute traces of this darkness. As we walked into the children's bedroom, something caught Paul's eye. He turned to Duna and said, 'Your daughter doesn't like that doll, does she?'

Duna nodded in agreement. 'Yeah,' she answered, 'She keeps saying it talks to her.' Patrick reluctantly picked the doll up and took it away to the rubbish bins at the back of the house. Somehow this evil force had managed to impregnate itself into this innocent doll, creating something that would not have been out of place in a horror movie. Finally, we scanned and removed any shards we could find from Mick and Duna's auras.

All that remained now was to exchange the energy in the whole block of flats and seal with a protective vibration that would stop it returning.

When we left, we were exhausted, yet it took a further ten minutes to remove all the debris we had collected in our own energetic field. So carefully planted for the future. We had learnt the hard way in the past. We were not going to make the same mistakes again. So no matter how tired we were, we checked and cleansed and then checked again.

Duna rang me a couple of days later to share what happened with the children. They had left them at Mick's mom's that night. So they did not return until the next day. She recounted how they had been reluctant to go back to the house. As soon as they entered the house, all three children had jumped with joy. 'It is clear, Mommy, its lovely here,' the eldest had stated. 'They have all gone, Mommy, the man isn't hanging from a rope in the bathroom any more and the evil thing is no longer in my dolls,' chimed the middle little girl.

In time Duna would move from here but for the time being her children would no longer be tormented. As for Mick, he was now a strong believer in ghosts.

Afraid to Tell the Truth

Cindi lived locally with her two daughters, who were aged fifteen and eighteen. While she had lived in the house for over ten years, it had been over the last two when they had begun to experience strange phenomena. Over time these had grown more intense and were now frightening them all. Yet Cindi was not able to explain what was happening to her.

She had called me on several occasions to ask for advice and assistance, but she seemed unable to give me any real, tangible evidence that could justify getting a team of four together to deal with something and nothing. On the second occasion, I asked Cindi to write anything down that happened over the next couple of weeks. If she had any frightening or negative experiences, she should log them and give me a call back. This technique often helps when there is some uncertainty concerning a suspected haunting. It often helped the person concerned. Sometimes at the end of a period, they could see that there had been nothing really untoward happening surrounding them.

This Cindi duly did, and she came back with a list. The television switching itself on and off, and several other electrical appliances were randomly operating on their own, such as, the kettle, the radio, and on one occasion, the vacuum cleaner. There appeared no logical explanation for this. A black shape, which grew in size from a small patch to a huge floating, rippling mass of mist, was seen on the top of the stairs and outside Cindi's bedroom. Both Cindi and her youngest daughter witnessed this strange phenomenon, which lasted several minutes. Both Cindi and the youngest daughter were experiencing almost identical nightmares, where a huge shadow, in the shape of a human being, would appear in their dreams. This figure was without features yet evoked terrifying fear in both on them. They had both, on separate occasions, woken up from their nightmarish experience quickly, only to experience a dark presence leaning over them and they would be unable to move. Bindi, the youngest, also experienced the sensation of her bed being violently shaken during the night.

Without doubt, I now had enough information and evidence to justify asking the others to give up another free evening to tackle this problem.

Lyn, Eddie, Patrick and I duly arrived on a bright, warm summer evening. As usual, I had told them nothing. I normally have a good idea what we will be attempting to deal with, but on this occasion, I wasn't entirely sure, but I was confident that as the evening unfolded, we would be shown what it was, in order that we could deal with it.

After polite preliminaries, we began the process of searching and scanning the ground floor of the property. Apart from a couple of dark patches in the bathroom, we could detect nothing.

On the first floor it was a very different story. Every room felt dark, fearful and intimidating. It was difficult to understand how this family had managed to sleep at night. Yet possibly the worst room of all was the bathroom. The eldest daughter, Bali, had begun to suffer from epilepsy and strangely enough, most of the attacks had happened in the bathroom.

As we swept the rooms, the two girls began to giggle, so did Mom, and the team started to get annoyed. It seemed as if they found the whole process funny. Our attempts to try and solve their problems, to all intents and purposes was a source of amusement to them. I looked across at Lyn and her eyes said it all. Who is going to address this, me or you? I decided to tackle the issue. I explained to Mom that I was more than willing to give up my time, but it was a little off-putting when the occupants found these supposedly frightening experiences comical. In a flash Cindi apologised and explained that they had been so frightened for so long, it was the relief that someone was actually trying to help them. Lyn was not convinced. Without words, I indicated I felt there was another cause for this inappropriate behaviour. Something was doing its damnedest to get rid of us. For a moment it would have been so easy to respond to this. Fortunately, in the nick of time, I realised what it was attempting to do.

We decided to start in the bathroom. White Feather urged me to separate the girls from Mom and use the female members of the team. I placed Patrick in the bedroom, located at the farthest point from the bathroom, while Cindi, Lyn, Eddie and I squashed ourselves into this small closet. With the room sealed, whatever was in here was going nowhere. We placed Cindi in the middle for protection and began to scan her and the room for an invisible presence. After a few seconds, in my mind's eye, I saw a winged creature rise up. It seemed to have been hiding deep in Cindi's vibration. Simultaneously, Lyn, who was positioned behind Cindi, pointed at her back. She was clearly showing me that there was something quite nasty attached to Cindi, without panicking Cindi herself. We both turned to Eddie, who calmly said she thought there was something in-between Lyn and Cindi. I thought for a moment. I turned Cindi towards me and asked her directly. "Cindi, have you ever experienced the sensation that something is having penetrative sex with you?"

There was no easy way to ask that question, other than being extremely direct. Cindi held my gaze for a moment. She appeared unsure how to answer the question. I held her gaze and looked at her. 'Yes,' she said, moving from foot to foot. I knew it, I sensed it, felt it. This was an Incubus at work.

Within seconds it was if an electric shock had surged through the room, it was angry and was determined to be as disruptive as it could be. So strong was the pulsation of energy, it almost appeared to send all our hearts racing. No one more so than Cindi, who began to say she couldn't breathe, she was clutching at her chest and her breathing was uneven; she was gulping breaths. Lyn, calmly and without saying a word, placed her hand on her back, as if to try and restabilise her. She asked a gentle 'Okay', as Cindi slowly began to gain control of her own breathing. After a few moments her breathing returned to normal. This thing was not going to give up easily, it now began to attack Cindi's mind. She became hesitant in continuing on with the clearance and was worried about the safety of her children and what this may conjure up and what it would do to her family after we had left and she was all alone in the house. I gently pointed out it would not go away, and she was aware it was after her girls next. I had said the magic sentence, a mom will in most circumstances place the safety and the good of her children above her own needs. It took Cindi a few moments to stabilise herself and place herself in a good space. 'Let's do this,' she said, and so we did.

It did not go without a fight. There were lots of lights dimming, changes in temperature and strange sounds which appeared to be coming from the very fibre of the house. But we won through, not before it made its mark. Before we left the room, Cindi asked us to look at her back: there were three deep scratches on either side of her back where blood had been drawn, seeping through her blouse.

Before we could leave, we had to convince her this was really gone. We all made our way to the lounge. In the corner we could hear a bird singing. Cindi removed a cover from the birdcage, and there was a rather bedraggled-looking bird singing its heart away. Cindi was in awe. She explained the bird had not sung in a long time, sometimes it screamed out in pain and cowered up in the corner in its cage.

We may not have been able to give any evidence her home was demon-free and finally her own again, but this little bird could, and it sang its heart away.